T0128944

Greenwich Village
TALES

CHUCK WALKO

authorHOUSE®

AuthorHouse™
1663 Liberty Drive
Bloomington, IN 47403
www.authorhouse.com
Phone: 1 (800) 839-8640

Published by AuthorHouse 12/21/2017

ISBN: 978-1-5462-2071-8 (sc)
ISBN: 978-1-5462-2070-1 (hc)
ISBN: 978-1-5462-2099-2 (e)

Library of Congress Control Number: 2017918859

Chapter One

JAMIE ROBERTS

"The weirdest trick I ever turned was Cicotti," said Jamie Roberts.

I thought this was a strange statement coming from Jamie Roberts because he was so weird himself.

"Ya know, Cicotti paid me fifty bucks once for takin' a shit on the glass coffee table in his living room while he laid on the shag carpet underneath. He was jerking off and looking up at the god damn glass coffee table while I shit a pile on his glass table top. And ya know what's even crazier. When I finished my dump I get up pulling my jeans up a bit careful not to mess his white shag as I head to the can to wipe myself, I see Cicotti squirting his cum like a fire hose."

"Did Cicotti say anything while all this was happening?" I asked.

"No, he didn't say nothing the whole time. But when I comes back into the parlor with a wad of toilet paper to clean off the table, guess what? The glass top is already clean as before I shit on it. Cicotti's dressed and looking smug as all hell sitting in his big lazy boy chair, acting like nothin' ever happened. I swear he must've used somethin' to scoop it up. Maybe he put it on a plate and put it in the frig for later." Jamie Roberts thought for a moment and then burst out laughing.

"Yep," Jamie said when his laughter subsided. "Cicotti really gives meaning to 'eat shit,' doesn't he?" Jamie took another long drag on his cigarette and then, as if thinking about his last statement as a kind of clever pun, grinned from ear to ear. "Imagine giving me fifty bucks to shit on his glass-top coffee table while he's under it wacking off."

"Did you ever go back for another fifty?" I asked.

"Hell, no!" Jamie responded. "That's too weird for me. I'll suck a guy's dick for fifty bucks or fuck him up the ass. I'll even let him fuck me for seventy-five, but taking a shit over a glass coffee table, no, that's too much. Cicotti asked me a few times after that, but I kept putting him off until he probably got the message. That Cicotti is one fucked-up weird dude."

I don't know whether Jamie Roberts was telling me the truth or he just made up this story of defecating in Sam Cicotti's living room to impress me. Jamie did have a reputation in the bar for exaggeration and attention seeking. I frequently saw him bragging to some of his male prostitute friends about the last john he had been with and what transpired between them. Of course, Jamie always had to tell anyone within hearing distance how much the john paid him. All the guys at the bar knew Jamie Roberts was never paid as much as he said he was.

I did not know if Jamie was aware of the fact that I knew Sam Cicotti not only from the bar, but that I indeed had been to his apartment on Fulton Street just a few weeks earlier. Jamie was telling the truth in that Sam really did have a coffee table with a glass top and he did have a white shag carpet. It's probably a good thing I heard Jamie's story after my visit. I probably would not have returned to the apartment on Fulton Street again, even though I enjoyed accepting Sam's invitation to play cards with him and have a few martinis. Sam worked in a mid-town accounting firm and seemed like a decent, if somewhat boring, man in his early forties. Other than some conversation about our jobs and how we came to live in New York, all we did was play some poker, have two martinis, and share a pipe of marijuana. There was not even a hint of doing anything of a sexual nature. Sam Cicotti did not seem to me to have any of the perversion that Jamie so enthusiastically related to me.

Concerning Jamie's claim of being paid fifty dollars from Cicotti I had my doubts, but I didn't confront Jamie with them. Even the good looking, preppy types and the well-built, movie star- wannabes who were meeting johns in bars like this one in pre-Stonewall Greenwich Village, New York, never earned the kind of money Jamie Roberts claimed. Through the grapevine I heard that a kid of Italian descent was hustling movie and TV older guys in a tie and jacket piano bar on the upper East Side. I heard he was getting as much as one hundred a trick and developing quite a reputation. He must have. Today that man is adored by a nation of women who see his every film; he's too old now for most gay men to show any interest. I understand that he has a marriage of convenience to a model thirty years his junior but keeps a boy who is in his early twenties.

When I first started going into the bar, Jamie tried to proposition me a few times, but after a while he must have realized that I was not interested in him. The funny and sad thing about our relationship was that I often thought that he truly liked me. The more I tolerated him, the more I think he grew fonder of me. I suppose it was because I was a bit fascinated by him, that he saddled up to me on a bar stool and told me stories while smoking his Lucky Strikes.

Jamie had a strange way of smoking. He held his cigarette in his right hand with his thumb on the right side of the cigarette, causing his hand to arch above his nose as he inhaled. He liked to blow out the smoke in circles and delighted when he could break the rings with his finger. I thought his manner of inhaling was an affectation to make him look tough, the blowing of the rings to look cool, and his breaking the smoke rings gave him a pathetic, little boyishness.

Perhaps Jamie Roberts looked at me as a big brother or father figure that he could talk to easily because I seldom gave any hint of denigrating him or telling him what I truly thought of him. Never once did I tell him to get lost, or tell him that he was weird, or call him a big- fucking liar. His sincerity and openness in a city of bull-shit artists was both amusing and genuine. The truth of the matter was that he was interesting to me; he was a real character and I thought of myself as an author in search of a character. He was also one of the few people who would start a conversation with me and keep it going- at least until a new, better looking man or a john would come into the bar. All it took Jamie to babble on was a few pointed, open-ended questions that I would ask in good journalistic style, which I was studying that semester.

My NYU professors would have been proud of my handling of Jamie Roberts.

I had no sexual interest in Jamie. Perhaps it was because he was - and no pun is intended here- queer-looking to me. I, at six feet-two, was slightly taller than Jamie, but he must have only weighed about 140 pounds, thus giving him a moth-eaten appearance. He had long, stringy hair that hung below his shoulders; his hair was obviously bleached because his eyebrows were brown and on most occasions, his brown roots could be seen beneath his matted blonde tresses. He had acne; it was obvious that he was squeezing pimples rather than treating them.

Wearing one's cap backwards had just become a fad because of Holden Caufield in **Catcher in the Rye**. Perhaps Jamie wished he were one of the N.Y.U. frat boys who tossed frisbees in Washington Square, so he too turned his cap backwards. Of course, it was red. Jamie was perhaps the first man I met who was exerting his individuality by accepting the norms and fads of his day, thus becoming the mass stereotype that later marked an entire generation.

At the time, I didn't know how old Jamie was; I just assumed he was only three or four years younger than I; but his appearance, conversations, and general mannerisms made him seem a lot younger. In many ways Jamie reminded me of the high school juniors I taught English to a year ago. This is probably why I was not interested in him physically. The other- greater reason- of course, was that I thought Jamie was homosexual and I wasn't.

Chapter Two

A LOOK BACK IN TIME

After a few minutes Jamie left me to feed the jukebox, and then he got into a conversation at the far end of the bar. I smiled to think of Jamie and the other guys who gathered here. The bar was like a home to many of them. It was a place where their lonely lives could connect over a problem or the day's events or even a dream of love. Here they were away from the reality of another world: a heterosexual world. For many the price of a beer was cheaper and better than a visit to a psychiatrist. By now I knew many of the men by face if not by name. On Fridays and Saturdays, the place was so packed with out-of-towners, it was almost impossible to talk above the din of a hundred conversations and blaring music; but on weekday afternoons before the five o'clock happy- hour, you could get to really know someone

As I gazed around the room and its neighborhood denizens, I thought back on my own life, how I managed to get to this place, and how my life had changed in just a few short months. I realized that I no longer was the stiff conservative living in the closet back in New Jersey. This time last year I wouldn't have even imagined that people like Jamie Roberts existed or that I would be having a friendly conversation with them. I knew they were all homosexuals and I enjoyed being here, and yet was still denying- or questioning- why I was here. Was I still as closeted as ever or was I waiting for the right moment- or guy- to get me out of denial? It was one thing to accept one's surroundings but it was harder to accept those events that brought one to a given point in life.

Looking at Jamie and his friends, I thought about those events that led me to this time and place.

In one of the longest continuously running plays in history, **The Fantastiks,** there is a song that seems appropriate here. That song, of course, is "Try to Remember." Most of these "tales" happened in the 1960's. A brief, kaleidoscopic reflection of that decade may be in order. And so.... to Remember.

In Rome there was the Second Vatican Council, which lasted three years and scanned two papacies. It was intended to modernize the Church but ended up causing more people to realize it was systemically antiquated, thus resulting in more people leaving the faith.

In Washington there was a new, young, Catholic president who was to epitomize an administration some would call "Camelot," but they disregard the Bay of Pigs, the Cuban missile crisis, or Vietnam "advisers." We developed the Peace Corps to improve humankind throughout the world. That dream ended in Dallas.

The world began to look beyond itself. In 1962 NASA sent the first planetary probe to Venus. The "space race" culminated on the moon with "One small step for man, one giant leap for mankind."

The new administration in Washington gave us the "War on Poverty" and the Civil Rights and Voting Rights Acts, but the poor continued to increase and the middle class began a slow disappearing act. Meanwhile, cities like Los Angeles, Detroit, and Newark were being destroyed by riots. Then in 1965 there was the Gulf of Tonkin and the "Tet Offensive." What was to be an advisory situation turned into one of the worst military, economic, and cultural fiascos in history.

The country met a charismatic Black man who had a dream and preached non-violence until he himself was assassinated.

From England came the Beatles. It was also the time of the Rolling Stones, and students of music seemed to abandon the classical and operatic for rock and roll and folk music.

The Age of Aquarius which promised peace and love turned into sit-ins, riots, and protests at Columbia University, U.C. Berkley, and killings at Kent State. The nation's intelligentsia read about and thoroughly discussed the "The Warren Report" and the "Pentagon Papers"; but the war, which was never officially called a war because Congress never declared it, continued on. Psychologists coined another term- post traumatic disorder or PTD, while drug use began to outdo the evils of Prohibition.

Color television came of age. The Super Bowl was born. The world heard the name 'Pele.' Ebbets Field, Sportsman's

Park, Crosley Field and others were torn down. A World's Fair was held in New York.

From the Netherlands the world began playing tape cassettes.

England gave us fiber optics.

It was the age of Existentialism, and the plays of Edward Albee and others portrayed this non-philosophy in the "Theater of the Absurd." Oscar Hammerstein passed away at the beginning of the decade. Theaters still managed to produce memorable dramas such as *A Taste of Honey, Becket, Camelot, Man of La Mancha, West Side Story* and *Evita*.

In New York cops were chasing the "fairies out of the bushes" in Central Park and "detaining" prostitutes around 42nd Street. Police around the country felt obliged to increase their numbers by attempting to enforce laws which were designed to control moral behaviors through government oversight. Ironically, however, despite these municipal endeavors, the number of homosexuals and prostitutes in cities such as San Francisco, Chicago, Philadelphia, Washington D.C., Los Angeles, and New York increased dramatically.

In New York City, so-called "gay" bars began to appear largely through the efforts of the mafia. There were specific bars for specific tastes: discos for the twenty-something, dress-up piano bars where suits and ties were required, "drag" bars for businessmen to meet transsexuals and other men wearing fashionable female attire and make-up, "leather" bars for those who preferred denim and "S and M" or sadomasochism. Different colored handkerchiefs in one's back pocket became a more direct form of introduction than 'are you a friend of Dorothy?' There were bars that were primarily frequented by Oriental, Black men or Puerto Ricans. There were "hustler" bars for those who preferred paying for sex with men of their choice rather than the female prostitutes. While there was an occasion police "raid" at one of these establishments, their number continued to increase. At one point there were three, large bath houses or popularly called "tubs" catering to homosexuals. One was well-known for the female entertainers who performed there, thus giving it a hip ambiance; another, seemed to cater to the "leather" crowd until it burned in a fatal tragedy.

Among the "after hours" places that sprung up were the deserted and decrepit piers and warehouses on Manhattan's West Side. Here men of all ages, types, and professions might venture into the early morning hours for indiscriminate sex in total darkness among the rats and human waste odors. This entire area would later be transformed into the beautiful and family-friendly Hudson River Park.

Greenwich Village became the mecca for homosexual men who were replacing the ethnic groups and artists and writers of previously decades. Similar transitions were taking place in the Castro of San Francisco, Hillcrest in San Diego, and South Beach in Florida. These transitions soon took on the more genteel architectural terms of "gentrification" and "art deco."

A student of history may conclude that the Stonewall Riots of June 1969 culminated in the homosexual revolution as much as Woodstock in August of the same year marked the "Sexual Revolution" for heterosexuals, drugs, peace and rock 'n roll. An anthropologist or philosopher may look at

Stonewall as that culminating incident which represents the realization of a human evolutionary process. With that realization, society was being forced to accept that human developmental process. It did not really start with Stonewall or Woodstock. They were merely the manifest incidents marking it.

As with any era, the 1960's represented great changes in technology, religion, the arts, and human nature. It was a decade of hope and despair. It was a period not unlike what Charles Dickens had much earlier described as "The best times, the worst of times." In years to come, historians may refer to the decade of the '60's as the "Age of Irony" for in each great new advancement in human growth there seems to have been a counter deficit.

After graduating from college with a degree in English literature, I taught in a suburban New Jersey high school for three years. During those years I went back to college every semester, including three full summers to earn a Master of Arts in English. My social life- particularly my sex life – was, it seemed to me on an ever- lasting hold during those years.

As an undergraduate, I dated a number of girls from school and a few of the young women I met during my summer jobs. During my junior year I met an art major that I fell in love with, and we saw each other on a daily basis. After our junior year, however, she went to work down the Jersey shore as a boardwalk sketch artist and met someone else. I really did not care about our breakup because she and the sex we were having was getting mechanical, if not boring, by that time. In my senior year, I began dating another English major. We had much in common and enjoyed one another's company. We saw each other at school every day, had lunch together every day, and went to all the college activities together. Her friends became my friends and vice-versa. Once a month for over a year, we went to New York City to see a Broadway play. We would stay in the city after the shows for dinner and to critique the play. On some occasions we would go away for an entire weekend either alone or with another couple or two.

All our friends were getting engaged and planned on getting married shortly after graduation. Back in the 1960's that seemed to be the typical pattern. Even though we did not get engaged, we continued to see each other once in a while for the next two years, but our busy work and study schedules reduced social events considerably and then to non-what-so- ever.

For me, however, the pattern did not seem right. Marriage was a permanent thing back then, certainly it was in the Roman Catholic culture in which I lived. Once you said "I do," you were expected to stay together and be faithful to that one person for the rest of your life. Another problem which I had with my religion was that one was not to have sex before marriage. I could not imagine marrying without knowing whether that person was sexually compatible. In the 1950's and '60s a girl who permitted a man to do more than kiss, fondle her breasts, and perhaps slip a hand into her panties was considered a tramp and not worth marrying anyway. And then, in my case, I had to run off and confess the sin to a chaste priest, or one whom I thought was chaste.

Divorce in my milieu was taboo if not unthinkable. I must admit that I was also very much a romantic who believed that eventually I would find the perfect princess; I would be her knight in shining armor, I would unlock her chastity belt, and together we would ride off into perpetual bliss. Since this did not happen, I continued to disillusion myself, friends, and family with the old line: "I haven't found the right girl yet, but I'm still looking."

While I had quite a few physical experiences with females from my days in college and graduate school, I never could see myself as being married to any of them. I simply could not experience the sexual passion that I thought necessary to sustain a relationship beyond the first month or so. All of the women I dated were physically beautiful, intelligent, and vivacious. Some were better during love making than others.

It seems in retrospect that I deliberately chose to date the best- looking women in college in hopes that they could keep me physically aroused in them, but inevitably after a short time the sex drive I felt waned quickly. I tortured myself into believing that if only my testosterone level were high enough, I could continue to have enjoyable sex with the same female partner until "death do us part." But it never seemed to work out that way, and once I started working and going to grad school, romantic ideas were really farther away.

At one point I thought I may have been homosexual, but gave that idea little thought because I went out with women and really liked the company of women. The few homosexuals I knew were very effeminate, a trait which then- as is the case to this very day- I do not care for. While I did enjoy the company of men, I thought that to be homosexual meant that you were effeminate. Indeed, I often referred to this type as "silly assed fairies." I certainly was not like that, so I deluded myself into believing that I could not possibly be homosexual.

I did have what may be considered a homosexual experience the summer after graduating from college. Seth Freeman, a college friend, who was the boyfriend of one of the girls in our clique, had invited me to visit him at the Jewish day camp he directed. The invitation was that I should meet him at the camp after 5:00 when it closed. He showed me around the various facilities before we decided to put on our bathing suits and go for a swim in the lake. We both had fun diving off the large wooden raft in the middle of the camp's lake. As the sun began to set, the temperature began to get a little chilly. Seth suggested that we take a shower, get dressed, and go out for dinner.

In the shower room we took off our bathing suits and Seth stood next to me even though there were six showers on each side of the room. After a while I noticed that he was messaging his penis and it was becoming erect. Perhaps because I was intrigued by this and didn't say anything, he was encouraged to reach for my penis and began messaging it. The sensation was pleasurable and exciting. After a while he turned off the cold water shower and got down on his knees to put my penis in his mouth. His tongue played around my cock as he moved it in and out of his mouth.

Instinctively, I leaned back against the wall of the shower and closed my eyes. It was a new and strangely exciting experience. Neither Seth nor I spoke, but I thought that Seth seemed to be enjoying his part more than any girl who had ever given me fellatio. The fact that he initiated the situation-that I didn't practically forced a girl to do it after she was greatly aroused, aroused me even more. I realized I was about to ejaculate and quickly pulled back as my semen spewed out across the floor of the shower room. I felt exhausted and confused. In silence I asked myself if what just happened, really did. Did Seth Freeman, whom I had known all year and went out with on double dates, whom I had seen kissing and petting his girlfriend, really perform this act on me? I did not speak, but did turn on the shower to wash off again and try to remove some cum off the floor.

Seth didn't say anything until we were both half dressed. "I hope you liked it as much as I did," Seth said. "We have to try it again real soon, okay."

As we walked back to the parking area to our cars, I made up an excuse for not going out to eat. He accepted my excuse with the understanding that he was going to call me in a few days. He did telephone me about four weeks later; he apologized for not calling sooner. When he asked if we could get together again, I made up an excuse. Our conversation ended with, "Okay, some other time then." I never saw or heard of Seth Freeman after that.

Chapter Three

MY MOVE AND DISCOVERIES

Because I wanted to further my education by earning a Ph.D., I studied for and took the Miller Analogy test and completed several entrance forms to various universities, and was thrilled when I got accepted into the program at New York University, my first choice. Because it had taken me so long to complete the master's degree, I vowed that I would study full time. I had saved for three years and with a teaching assistantship would be able to pay tuition and living expenses for at least two years.

In June of 1965, I rented a small, but cheap, apartment on 10th Street in Greenwich Village. My fourth floor walk-up apartment had three rooms and a bath. The rental agent told me that I was lucky to get such a spacious apartment so close to Washington Square at such a cheap rental. She explained that all the units in the building were exactly the same; there were two on each floor. The rent was less because this was on the fourth floor and there was no elevator. The agent said that this was the only vacancy and I better take it immediately, because if I waited even a few hours it would be taken. She added that later in August the college students would be grabbing any apartment in the Village that they could find at twice the rental price. I signed a year's lease and gave her a deposit check. She in turn, gave me the key. I was thrilled to have my own place and to be living in the Village, where I could walk to my classes at the University. I was twenty- four years old and filled with the excitement of beginning a new phase of my life.

I looked around the bare apartment. It had two entrance doors; one was into the living room which was in the front facing 10th Street.; the other entrance was into a small foyer off the kitchen which was in back of the building. The bath room was directly across the entrance door into the kitchen. The bedroom was between the living room and the kitchen. There was a small closet built into the corner of the room, but there was no window in the bedroom.

It was then that I realized I would have to furnish this apartment as much as possible and would have to lug whatever furniture I was able to get up the four flights of stairs. Suddenly, my enthusiasm over the place began to fade. But it was too late: I was accepted into NYU, I quit my teaching job in New Jersey, sold my car to help pay some of the new expenses, and signed a year's lease; but I would be living in New York, the City I loved. "Make the most of it, Cee Jay," I said aloud to myself. "This is it. There's no turning back now."

The next week was busy getting my schedule of classes and familiarizing myself with some faculty, their offices, and class locations as well as purchasing books. I learned where the grocery store and laundry were, and I had the electricity turned on as well as a telephone installed in the living room. My rental agent told me where I could buy a few pieces of inexpensive furniture and have them delivered up to 4-A. My apartment now had a futon sofa, a double bed, and a kitchen table with four chairs. For the next year or so that table would also serve as a desk.

My sister and brother-in-law drove in from New Jersey with some "house-warming" gifts. These were all used, hand-me-downs but much needed and welcomed items. We struggled up the front stoop and the four flights of stairs several times with a set of dishes, glasses, silverware, towels, window shades and drapes for the living room. They also brought from my old apartment a radio, typewriter, black and white television, and a few reference books. In between our trips up and down the stairs, we celebrated my new life with a bottle of wine which they brought.

Apartment 4-A was beginning to take shape. The television set was placed on the big box that contained the towels, curtains, and glasses. I put it in front of a sealed fireplace that had been covered with a tin protector. The marble mantle became a book shelf. Another box would serve as a temporary coffee table. Since I now had a bed, I could now start sleeping in my new apartment. I had been making trips to New Jersey each day not only for sleeping but to carry suit cases of clothes and other items.

The summer session began during the second week of July. The Friday of that week was overcast, humid, with on and off drizzle. Fortunately, I had taken an umbrella because as I walked to 10th Street from the University it began pouring about 4:00. The umbrella did not protect my shoes from the puddles and street splashes. By the time I got home my shoes and socks were dripping.

When I unlocked the door into the lobby, I noticed a man about my age sitting on the stairs. I went first to my mailbox. As I stood at the boxes pretending to be checking the few pieces of mail I received, I was thinking of the person sitting on the steps. I would have to pass him to get upstairs. I did not know him and immediately became apprehensive about seeing him in such a strange position. *At least he's not hiding in the darker halls up stairs to mug me,* I thought, *but what is he doing sitting there? Is he okay?* He was clean shaven and wore jeans. His dark brown hair was in a crew cut which seemed to compliment his brown eyes. Finally, I gathered the courage to turn around and face him as I approached the stairs.

He was the first to speak. He gave me a pleasant smile. "You must be the new tenant in 4-A," he said extending his hand. "My name is Paul Cresetto. I live in 3-A, right under you."

We shook hands as I gave him my name.

"I'm pleased to meet you, Paul. But why are you sitting on the steps here?"

"Good question!" he joked. "Because I'm stupid?" he said this as a possible answer to the question. "I went to D'Agostino's Market to get a few items for dinner tonight and left the keys in my apartment. I didn't realize it until I tried opening the door to the apartment. My roommate usually gets home around 5:30, but if he has extra work may even be later. he usually calls though to let me know if he will be late. So here I am without a phone to call him, soaking wet clothes, and some perishable food items. Stupid, Huh?" he paused. "But at least I got to meet my upstairs neighbor." Paul Cresetto's self- deprecation seemed charming in a way.

"Well, Paul, if you want, you can come up to my place. I don't have much furniture, but the refrigerator is working and I have a telephone you may use."

"Thank you. That will be great!" As he stood up to get his bags, I noticed that he was barefooted; he picked up a pair of very wet sandals.

On the way up to 4-A, I told him that I had moved from New Jersey, and he told me that his roommate was also from the Garden State, and he was originally from Wisconsin. They lived in 3-A for two years. Inside the apartment the first thing we did was put his food items in the refrigerator. I offered him a beer which he accepted and we moved into the living room. We both sat on the futon, which was the only piece of real furniture in the room.

"It's really good of you, Cee Jay., to let me come in here. I appreciate it. I can't believe I did a stupid thing like leaving my keys in the apartment. You know this isn't the first time either. About a year ago I did the same thing. George, that's my roommate, George Miller is his name, He's gonna rib me about this forever."

I pointed out the telephone, which was on the floor under one of the windows, and told him that it was okay to call his roommate. When he called he did not tell George the full story but did emphasize that he should come home as soon as possible. He told him that he was in the apartment over theirs.

"That's right, 4-A,' he said. "Yes, that's right… our new neighbor. …Yes, he is good looking … No, not as good looking as you. … Of course not! …His name? …He prefers to be called 'Cee Jay.' Now for God's sake, will you get your ass home as soon as you can. …Yes, I'll still be in Cee Jay's apartment, so call me as soon as you get home … Oh, you need his number." He turned toward me. "Is it okay if I give Dip-shit your telephone number?" I nodded yes.

"Well, what is it?" he asked. As I gave him each number, he repeated it into the phone. When he finished, he repeated the whole number again as if reassuring himself that he had it memorized and that George had written it down correctly. "Okay, I'll see you soon. …Yes, I love you too. Bye."

When he returned to the futon, he again thanked me for using the phone.

"Oh, that's okay. Any time." I smiled. "It must be nice to call your roommate a 'dip shit' and tell him that you love him all in the same sentence."

Paul chuckled. "When you know someone as long as George and I have, it's okay to kid around like that." His tone changed. "But I really do love him."

"You told me that you were from Wisconsin. How long have you known one another?"

"We met at Rutgers, New Brunswick. That was eight years ago, but we didn't really get to know one another very well. George was a year ahead of me. We met again by accident three years ago here in New York. It was in New York that we really got to be friends. We decided to move in together two years ago. And yes, I know what you're thinking, so yes, we are…as they say…. friends of Dorothy."

I had never heard the expression 'friends of Dorothy' before and I told him so.

"Where have you been all your life? In a convent? Let me give you a hint: you know…Dorothy… from Kansas….the Wizard of Oz…. Judy Garland."

The expression on my face may have been of bewilderment.

"If you don't know what it means stay in the Village another week, Honey. You'll know the expression real soon." Almost as to change the subject, Paul said. "May I use your bathroom?"

"Of course," I said. "It's in the….."

"I know, off the kitchen. Same as my place."

When Paul returned he asked me why I moved to the Village.

He told me that he was a teacher also. He worked in a private, junior high school on the upper west side of Manhattan. He said that he had stayed at Rutgers University to get his master's degree in educational administration, but had no thought at present of going beyond the M.A. He enjoyed traveling and after working with junior high kids during the year, just wanted to unwind and do nothing in particular. He and roommate George were planning a windjammer cruise to the Caribbean in late August. Paul told me that George was an attorney for the American Civil Liberties Union.

I enjoyed talking to Paul. He was friendly and had a casual attitude. We discovered that we were both twenty-four. Time passed quickly as we each recounted humorous incidents in our teaching careers. The rain had stopped.

When the phone rang, without hesitation, Paul picked it up. As expected, George told him that he was now home and Paul should come down stairs.

Paul thanked me again for using my refrigerator, and said, "…taking this poor wet, waif into your home." He left barefooted and carrying his bags as well as the wet sandals.

About an hour later my telephone rang. It was Paul inviting me to come down to his apartment to have dinner with him and his roommate George. "It's my way of again thanking you for taking me in this afternoon. "Besides, George wants to meet you," he added. "Nothing fancy. Just spaghetti and meatballs. It's my Italian cooking non-specialty," he said. "I hope 7:30 isn't too late for dinner for you."

I told him that since I didn't have much in the 'frig' and was thinking of going out to a restaurant, I would be happy to visit with him and George. The truth of the matter was that I was anxious to see what his apartment was like, and to meet his roommate, George. I wondered if these two men could possibly become my friends. We were the same age and lived in the same building. It would be nice having friends in the city other than the professors and fellow students at the University.

George Miller opened the living room door when I knocked. We warmly shook hands. George was about my height and weight. He had bright blue eyes and a full head of bushy light brown, almost blonde hair. The five-o'clock facial stubble gave him a masculine, model look. He wore cut-off shorts and a white polo shirt which augmented his muscled arms and abs. He wore sandals similar to those that Paul wore that afternoon. He was, as Paul said, very good looking.

"Hi, Cee Jay," Paul yelled from the kitchen. "I'll be out in a minute. Hope you're hungry!"

"That I am!" I called back.

"George, make our guest a drink. He likes martinis, so make three of them," Paul called.

"Please sit down," George said motioning to one of the two chairs facing the large leather sofa. "May I make you a drink?"

"Yes, thanks," I said.

George Miller went over to a small portable bar which they had in the corner. "Olive or lemon peel? How do you like your poison? On the rocks or straight up?" He paused. "Paul told me that you are from New Jersey. Did he tell you that I'm originally from New Jersey also?"

"Yes, he did. He also told me that he was from Wisconsin, but you met at Rutgers"

"Well, I went to the University of Wisconsin and played football for my freshman year, but I also wanted to play baseball; so I moved back to New Jersey. I was born and raised in Bayonne, New Jersey."

Suddenly, I was surprised. His name at first seemed vaguely familiar, but it was a common name. Also, when I first meet him he looked familiar, but now the pieces fit, and the expression on my face must have given me away.

"Is something wrong?" George asked as he handed me a large martini glass.

"I think we met before," I said. "You went to Saint Benedict's Prep in Newark, didn't you?"

"Yes, I did. Class of '59. How did you know I went to Benedict's?"

"Because I graduated in 1960 from the Prep."

"Wow, you must have a good memory to recognize me after all those years."

"Well, you were very popular in high school. You probably don't remember this, but I interviewed you for an article in the school paper when you were named valedictorian of your class. You also got the scholar/athlete award that year. You were a quarterback in football and a great baseball pitcher too."

"Wow, that's amazing! How coincidental! I sure do remember the article. I still have it in an album back home. My mother is very proud of it and often said how well written it was. I am sorry, though, that I didn't remember you. Now I can thank you for all the kind things you said about me back then." George reached his glass to mine and a slight ting was made.

"You couldn't remember me because I was a lowly junior and not into sports. I was more into newspaper and the creative writing club. Sort of nerdy, I guess. I did see you play in the football game against Seton Hall Prep on Thanksgiving. And I often saw you around the school, particularly in the cafeteria. I know you were outstanding as a baseball player, but must admit that I never saw a game. Sorry!"

Just then Paul came into the living room. "What am I missing in here, guys?" he asked.

"Cee Jay and I went to the same high school in Newark," George said enthusiastically. "He remembers writing an article about me in the school paper. How's that for coincidence, dear?" He got up and walked over to the bar and handed Paul the drink which he had made for him.

"All kinds of coincidences are happening today," Paul said. He sat next to George on the leather sofa, and ruffled his hand through his roommate's hair. "Tell me, Cee Jay, was Dip-shit here as good looking in high school as he is today?"

"Oh, even more so," I said. The three of us laughed.

"Don't let that go to your head, big guy," Paul said to George. Then he turned to me. "You know when I first met George, it was love at first sight."

Paul's blunt statement of love took me by surprise. It must have also embarrassed George because he immediately got up and changed the subject. "Well, why don't we finish our drinks in the kitchen. I'm starved," George said.

On the way to the kitchen, we had to pass through the bedroom. George led us out of the living room and began opening the second of the French doors which separated the kitchen from the bedroom. I could not help but notice that there was just one big bed in the room. I immediately realized that these two men were actually sleeping together. This thought occupied my mind briefly. Opposite the bed was a large dresser and mirror.

Paul drew my attention to a picture on the dresser. It was of a baseball team, and printed above the picture were the words; "Scarlet Knight Baseball 1963."

"Can you pick us both out?" Paul asked.

I quickly scanned the photo. It was easy to spot both of them because other than wearing their baseball uniforms, they had not seemed to change much. Paul was pleased that I was quickly able to spot them and picked up another framed photograph at the other end of the dresser. "This picture was taken in Acapulco two years ago. We went there for our first anniversary." The picture was of the two of them in bathing suits on what seemed to be a cruise boat with the Mexican beach in the background. They had their arms around one another and were smiling broadly. They both looked very happy; their suntans and the lighting added to their handsome appearance.

As I put the picture down, I turned to the bed. "Wow!" I exclaimed. "Somebody is a baseball fanatic in this house." Pinned on the wall over the bed were literally dozens of pennants from various colleges and major and minor league teams.

"I must amuse him," Paul said. "He needs just a few more to complete the majors. When that happens, down they come from our bedroom. He can put them in the rec room when we get our house. Honestly, he's like a little boy with his collection."

The kitchen was another surprise. They had fashioned a large drapery from the wall by the hall to the entrance and bathroom and then another drape hung from the left wall across the room to the right wall, thus creating an intimate dining area.

"What a great idea," I said. "Who's the decorator here?"

"Actually, we are both responsible for this one," George said. "Whenever we have guests for dinner or want a little coziness ourselves, we pull the curtains closed. That way we don't have to look at our old stove, sink and refrigerator. It gives the place a more charming ambiance," he added by lighting two votive candles on the cloth covered table.

"Please. Sit down. I'll get the chianti," he said going behind the curtain.

Paul already had set the table with glasses, silverware, etc. I was impressed how elegant it all seemed. I had never done anything like this with men before. George returned with the wine and poured our glasses before sitting down. He reached for Paul's hand on his left and Paul simultaneously reached for my hand. I took George's lead by bowing my head in what seemed a moment of silent prayer. "Now, let's eat," he said.

Our first course consisted of a tasty salad with finely diced mushrooms. Warm rolls were placed on the table with a heaping bowl of pasta. For dessert we had ice cream. We finished the bottle of chianti.

During the meal, I asked George why he went to Wisconsin to attend college. He told me that he was awarded two scholarships, one for academics which went for tuition and the other was a sports scholarship for room and board. "I had a free college ride for four years. Wisconsin- Madison was the only college that offered me such a complete package. Seton Hall University and Rutgers both offered good scholarships, but I wanted to get as far away from an over-protective Catholic mom and conservative, stereotypical dad as possible," he explained. "By the time senior year in high school came, I knew that I was a homosexual and wanted to get way so I could start a whole new life. Playing football for the Badgers was more than I could handle and... believe it or not... I was homesick for Jersey and also wanted to play baseball, which I preferred."

"I was on the baseball team with George during his junior and senior years at Rutgers," Paul offered. "I joined the team as a sophomore; George was a junior. We never really got to know one another though. He was a pitcher and I played infield, mostly short stop."

He stopped to chuckle. "Would you believe, once the coach actually said to me that if I watched the batter more than the pitcher, I might be a better player. Unfortunately, George graduated before I did, and we hardly spoke privately during those two years."

"I was out but very secretive about it then," George said. "No one on the team even suspected that I was queer. Certainly Paul didn't let me know. I didn't even know about that comment the coach made to Paul until last year. Had I known, I would definitely would have made it with Paul sooner."

"How and when did you guys get together then?" I asked.

Paul answered my question. "By accident we ran into one another in La Bar three years ago. Dip shit didn't even remember me, so I practically had to spell out the whole story of playing with him at Rutgers. After graduation he went to law school and got the job with the ACLU after passing the bar exam. I always wanted to live and work in Manhattan, so that's how I got here. We were both living and working in the City for a few years before we met."

George continued their story. "The night we met, we quickly went back to his place and did some wild, wicked fornicating. We both came about four times before we stopped only to go out for breakfast in the morning. After that it was telephone sex and talk every weekday night. We got together for the weekends either at his place or mine. Sometimes we would go away for the weekend like to Fire

Island or New Hope, Pennsylvania. After a year we decided that it was time to move in together so we took this place. We've been here two years now and saving to buy a house together out of the city. We both like the Buck's County area of PA or Frenchtown area of New Jersey. I would like to have a small, private law practice."

"So there you have our whole story," George said. "Now Cee Jay, tell us about yourself. We know you're doing graduate work at NYU. I know you went to Saint Benedict's for high school."

"There's really not too much to tell that you already don't know," I said.

"Paul told me that he didn't know whether or not you were gay. So, are you?"

George's question was so direct and sudden, I did not know how to respond. After a few seconds of silence which seemed like minutes to me, I feebly responded. "I really don't know what I am, to tell the truth. All I can tell you is I'm twenty-four years old and not married. I've had a few girlfriends along the way and had two sexual encounters that didn't mean much with men. This may sound crazy to you, but you two are the first men I have ever met that actually live together as lovers. I never even thought it was possible that two nice guys like you could live such a way. Being here tonight is a real eye- opening experience for me. You have introduced me to a whole way of life I never thought possible before." I paused. "And I really like it," I added. "Thanks guys." I lifted my now empty wine glass as a toast.

"Thank you for opening up to us like that," George said. "Now let's talk about baseball. Paul and I still play on La

Bar's team. The clubs in New York and New Jersey support teams that play in leagues. Most of our games are played on Saturday morning or afternoons in New Jersey. We get together in a park in the center of a town called Bloomfield, right off the Garden State Parkway. We'll be playing there next Saturday, and you can come with us to watch the game. You and Diane can be our cheerleaders. Most of the people who stand around and watch us in the park have no idea we are all gay and represent gay bars."

I interrupted. "Who is this Diane that you just mentioned?"

"That's right," Paul answered. "You haven't had the pleasure yet of meeting Diane. She's our resident fag hag who lives in 2-B."

"What's a fag hag? I asked.

"Honey, you really got to get with the lingo, if you're going to make it in the Village," Paul said. "A fag hag is a woman who for any number of reasons prefers the company of gay men. Diane is like our big sister. She's great to pal around with at clubs; we love to go shopping with her. You'll meet her soon enough. Everyone on the La Bar's team loves Diane. She has a really foul mouth for the other teams."

"You have mentioned this place- this "The Bar" a few times," I said. "What is it?"

"It's a neighborhood gay bar," George said. "You probably passed it many times already and didn't know about it. It's just around the corner. It's one of the oldest and best known bars in New York."

"Honey, let's take Cee Jay there tomorrow night."

"Sure, if he is willing to give it a look-see, we can both take him there." George turned to me. "Paul and I met there and we play on its team, but we seldom, if ever, go there anymore. It's a good place to meet just about any type of man there is. Everyone seems to bop in and out of La Bar. By the way, that is the real name of the place: 'La' Bar."

"So, is it a date then for tomorrow night?" Paul asked.

"Sure. Why not? I have nothing to lose except maybe my virginity," I joked.

I went to bed that night please that I had met two interesting men and felt confident that we would become good friends. I was beginning to feel really good about living in 4-A and was looking forward to tomorrow night when I would go with Paul and George to my first gay bar.

Chapter Four

LA BAR

My neighbors were right. I had passed La Bar several times without realizing it. Except for a small, tiffany-type glass window in the front door that said in scroll "La Bar," there was no sign or marking on the otherwise solid wooden door. When I pointed the name out to Paul, he joking replied, "You are now entering la la land."

A haze of smoke seemed to cling in the air, making visibility difficult. We were standing near the front entrance, which was on a corner, for only a minute when someone came up to greet us. "George, Paul, how are you guys? I haven't seen you two in this place in a while. What have you been up to, as if I didn't know," he jabbed George with his elbow and laughed.

"We're showing our friend, Cee Jay here what the Village is truly like," George said. "Cee Jay, this is Juan, Juan, Cee Jay." The two of us shook hands. "Juan is from Puerto Rico and one of the greatest catchers in all of baseball," George said.

Juan smiled broadly. "Ah, Georgie, you too kind." Turning to me he said, "I'm only the second best catcher in the world. But Georgie, he the greatest pitcher." Juan winked at me. "Now Paulie here, he da worst short stop in history. Ain't that so, Paulie?" He laughed at his own comment.

"Well, we'll see about how good we all are next Saturday. You are going to be behind the plate for me, aren't you, Juan?"

"Sure. You bet, boss. I catch for you, and we beat those Asbury Park faggots, okay. You play, too, Cee Jay? You gonna play for La Bar?"

"No, I…."

"George spoke for me. "Cee Jay will be at the park. He's going to be a cheerleader."

"So, wha' happen to that bitch, Diane? She die? I should be so lucky."

"Diane will be there, Juan," Paul said. "Cee Jay will be there to make sure you and Diane don't kill one another."

"I hate that bitch," Juan directed his comment to me. "She's a prejudiced cunt!"

"Don't mind Juan, Cee Jay," Paul said jokingly. "He's just sore because Tom, our centerfielder gives her more attention than he does to Juan. Isn't that right, Juan?"

Juan turned his head and imitated spitting on the floor. "Straight guys shouldn't be allowed to play on all-gay baseball teams," he said angrily. "Well, nice meeting you, Cee Jay. We see you next Saturday in Bloomfield. You cheer loud for us and boo those faggots from Asbury Park. Okay, boss?" We shook hands again, and he was off to cruise the bar.

To our left were three large kegs in front of a long wooden bench. A few benches were positioned around the kegs. George spotted an empty space at one of the kegs and suggested that Paul and I sit there while he went to the bar to get our drinks. Paul told him that he would just have a MGD, which I later learned was Paul's beer of choice. "Martini or beer for you, Cee Jay?" George asked. When I said that I would prefer a martini, George responded, "Good man! You're on my team."

While George was getting our drinks, Paul and I scanned the full length of the bar. To our left against the wall was a stove; an over-sized man wore a white apron and hat was flipping hamburgers. Steam rose from his spatula as he pressed the meat against the greasy stove. The smell of grease mingled with the smells of smoke and pine sol permeated the area. "Believe it or not," Paul said, "they really make great burgers here. With potato salad or chips, really big dill pickles, and all the fixing you want, they're also the best bargain in the Village. They're served on paper plates with plastic knives and forks, but they're really big and juicy. After a win, George and some of the team come here to celebrate. There's nothing better than a couple of cold beers and La Bar cheese burger on a hot afternoon.

"In the back, up those stairs, is a little room with tables and chairs where you can go to eat or just talk privately with someone. I've seen guys in there sketching. Some actually write poems and stuff on the napkins on the red and white plastic table clothes. I've been told that Albee got the idea for "Who's afraid of Virginia Woolf" back there.

"Interesting!" I said. I noticed that George was talking to the bartender and pointing to us as though he were telling the short, elderly man where we were sitting. The bartender waved to Paul and me.

George placed the drinks on the keg in front of us and took one of the benches to sit on facing us. "Mario makes a real good martini here, Cee Jay. I pointed you out to him so that when he's working and you order a martini, he'll make it with Tanqueray rather than the well shit they call gin in here. The baseball team members also get drinks at half price, so I was sure to tell him that you will be playing with us."

"So, what do I owe you?" I asked.

"Nothing. You can get the next round. "He lifted his glass to touch mine and Paul's bottle as if making a toast. "Here's to Cee Jay discovering La Bar." We drank to that.

"What do you think of this place," George asked after a moment. "Seedy enough for you?"

"It's certainly interesting," I said.

"You won't hear any Bach or Beethoven in here," Paul said. "But you really will meet a lot of characters in this place. Stick around here a while and you will see all of 'hu-MAN-ity' come in here. That's what I like about this place. The diversity."

"Notice that he emphasized 'man' in 'humanity,'" George pointed out.

"Yes, diversity with cocks," Paul retorted. "This isn't the best cruise bar in town, but once in a while you might meet a dip shit like my lover here and the bells will go off. Any way, they did for us."

I noticed the wire-backed stools around the old, wooden bar. Huge mirrors in big wood frames were over the bar. Most of the men were standing around talking in groups of two or three. All the stools were occupied and few guys were leaning against the bar talking to those on the stools. A few were facing away from the bar, eyeing everyone else in the place. I saw a large juke-box in the far right corner. A few guys who looked too young to be in a bar were milling around the juke box. I thought that they would make a nice picture for a Norman Rockwell painting. I told this observation to George and Paul who seemed to think it rather funny.

"Those fine young men, as you call them, are hustlers," Paul said. "I doubt Norman Rocker would be interested."

"Hustler?" I questioned. "As in pool halls?"

"Not quite," George remarked. "These hustlers are after money all right, but they get it in exchange for sex from guys-mostly older gay, lonely men- who pay them. Some straight men also prefer sex with a young hustler than with their own wives. In here, Cee Jay, just about anything goes. But, if you want art, word has it on good authority that there is a real Leroy Neiman hanging on the wall in the dining room."

It was time for me to get the second round of drinks, so I took the small serving tray that Mario had given George and headed to the middle of the room. I introduced myself to Mario; we shook hands. "You're with Paul and George, aren't you?" I responded positively. Mario said, "That's one Miller genuine draft and two Tanqueray martinis on the rocks with twists. Right?"

"Right you are," I said, surprised that the only bartender in this busy place would remember what we ordered. As I waited for the drinks, I took a closer look at my environment. To the far right, passed the bar there was an old pay phone on the wall. I noticed that one of the hustlers had gone over to it and was trying to place a call. A large, picture window occupied the wall to the right. A brass rail on the wooden rail separated the window from the wall. To the right of the window were racks of magazines and newspapers. A cork bulletin board with various notes attached was over the racks.

When Mario came back with the drinks, I asked him how much I owed. "That'll be five bucks," he said. I gave him one five and a single. "One's for you," I said. He thanked me and then pulled a string which was attached to a large brass bell on the counter. I had heard this bell before, but just then realized it signaled a tip. As I turned away from the bar to return to my friends, I noticed that the man sitting on the stool next to me was a good looking middle- aged man. He was wearing a suit jacket and tie. We politely smiled to one another without saying a word.

A few minutes later I asked the guys where the men's room was. "Well, I wouldn't recommend it, but I guess if you really got to go, you really got to go," Paul said. "The décor and aroma in there are tres turn-of-the century." He directed me to a door near the side entrance and the area of the juke box.

The rest room was very small; it probably was converted from a closet. Paul was right about the décor. A small sink was hanging precariously from the wall. The urinal was a massive piece of porcelain. There was one stale in the room but it appeared occupied. The wooden walls were scratch with all kinds of graffiti and various names. The odor was a mixture of urine and pine sol. It almost made me gag.

I got out of there as quickly as I could, but as I was leaving, I bumped into a tall, skinny young guy with acne and long blonde hair protruding from a red cap turned backwards. He was going in. He gave me a smile and simply said, "How's it going, dude?"

"Oh, it's going, all right," I said sarcastically in return.

"I've seen cleaner cesspools than that men's room," I told my friends when I returned.

"You can't say I didn't warn you," Paul admonished.

We left shortly after that. I could tell that Paul and George were getting bored, and the bar was getting crowded. It was after ten thirty, which was my bedtime, so it was I that suggested we leave.

In the weeks and months that were to follow I became closer to Paul and George. I confided in them and they in me. I went with them and Diane to Bloomfield where they played baseball. On a few occasions the four of us got together for dinner or to play cards.

Diane and I became closer when we discovered our love of poetry and movies. Sometimes Diane and I would go out together without Paul and George.

One night, George, Paul, and I stayed up very late playing cards, talking, and drinking. I got quite intoxicated. As I was leaving their apartment, I grabbed both of them in a bear hug, and said that I really loved both of them. I really did! Tears welled in my eyes as I said it again. This gay couple was the first time I ever confessed loving a man.

I went to La Bar on my own a few times and enjoyed the company of the men I met there. I felt at home and accepted there. Perhaps for the first time in my life I was able to be, act, and speak my own self without compromise. I did have a few sexual encounters with men, but none of them lasted more than once.

I missed Paul and George during the ten days they were on their windjammer cruise, but they came back with stories and slides which they were anxious to share with Diane and me.

George went home to Bayonne, New Jersey, over the long Thanksgiving weekend and Paul flew out to Madison to be with his parents and brother. Diane and I went to a restaurant together for Thanksgiving dinner and on Saturday night we went to the Café Wha. I spent most of the weekend, however, alone reading and writing papers that were going to be due shortly.

Before Christmas, George and Paul gave a Christmas party. Diane was the only female at the party. I think the entire baseball team was there as well as a few of the other faces I had seen over time at the bar. They served a great buffet and the liquor flowed. They had decorated a beautiful tree and we sang songs and told jokes and stories; some were rather risqué. The party ended very late, but everyone had a great time.

When I was the only one left in the apartment, George broke down crying and told me that he hated the thought of going home for Christmas. He told me that his parents did not approve of his lifestyle and never wanted to have anything to do with Paul. Paul, on the other hand, had a family that was very accepting of his being homosexual, but Paul still preferred being in New York with his lover than going back to Wisconsin. He said that instead of his going home, he might send his younger brother, who had just started college that fall, the fare for him to fly to New York over the holidays.

As it turned out, George went to Bayonne early on Christmas morning, went to mass with his mother, and came back that evening. Paul did give his brother the Christmas present he most wanted: A trip to 'The Big Apple.' Sal Cresetto came from Wisconsin on December 24 and flew home on January 2. The four of us went to all the tourist attractions we could get to during the week. Sal was particularly interested in the music scene in the Village. Even in Wisconsin, he had heard of our Sunday afternoon 'circles' and 'the day the music stopped,' so we took him to Izzy Young's and The Village Gate, The Bitter End, and The Gaslight each night.

The four of us had a good New Year's Eve party at home in 3-A. While George and Paul were kissing at midnight, I felt awkward, so Sal and I jokingly embraced, said, "Oh, why the hell not" and kissed, rather passionately even though I knew he was straight. …. I thoroughly enjoyed meeting Paul's younger brother.

I started the new year confident about my future life and my studies and career. I had been introduced to many new people and experiences and was looking forward to a great new- and happy- year.

Chapter Five

TIM DONNELLY

My first impression of Tim Donnelly was that he looked like a bird that had just fallen out of its nest. He was so youthful looking, clean shaven, and neat that he seemed out of place in a bar like this. He was wearing light tan pants and a brown tweed jacket with leather elbow guards. His pale pink shirt was unbuttoned at the neck. If he wore a tie, he could easily be mistaken as a graduate assistant at N.Y.U. The really outstanding feature of Tim was his eyes; they were a light blue that seemed to be piercing through you with a sad, downcast pall. I found it difficult to look straight at him because of his eyes. If they were part of a woman's face, they might be considered beautiful; with Tim they only seemed to add to his naivete.

"Hello, my name is Tim," he said to me as soon as he came over to where I was sitting. He extended a warm and slightly moist hand to shake.

Boy this guy's direct, I thought as I introduced myself. "People in here know me as Cee Jay."

"Mind if I sit here?" he asked referring to the empty stool next to me.

"Please do."

"I'd use a stupid pick up line," Tim said after sitting down, "like 'Do you come here often?' but I know you do."

I gave a perplexing smile before responding. "How do you know... or presume to know... I come here often? Which, by the way, is not correct if you think two or three times a month is often."

"I'm sorry," Tim said lowering his voice and looking terribly apologetic. "I guess that I thought you might come here often because I saw you here last Saturday and now that I'm here again on another Saturday, so are you."

"You saw me here last Saturday. I don't remember meeting you."

"Well, we didn't exactly meet," Tim explained. "I couldn't get near you. You seemed to be deep in conversation with some kid with long blonde hair. There were no empty stools near you, and the entire bar was very crowded. I was standing over by the juke box, but I kept watching you." It was then that I noticed how piercing and sad his eyes were. "You're the reason I came back here tonight."

I must admit that I was so startled and flattered by this admission that I almost fell off my seat. I had never heard a man say anything quite so complimentary to another man. If he hadn't said it so sincerely, I might have thought that he was continuing his unusual pick up conversation.

"Thank you," I said after a momentary hesitation, "but why." I emphasized the 'Why?'

"I'm not sure why," Tim said thoughtfully. "Perhaps it's because you seem kind of normal, you don't smoke, you don't drink very much, you seem intelligent, I like the way you smile, the way you dress… Should I go on?"

"Yes! I'm loving all this flattery," I admitted jokingly.

"Okay. You're about my age, you don't seem to be a hustler, you don't seem to be a criminal, you look as though you shave and shower daily. I think you're handsome… and sexy."

"Wow!" was the only word I could think of saying. I really didn't know if this guy Tim was just putting me on or really meant what he had said. His manner of saying these things about me certainly was sincere. I felt that I wanted to get to know him a lot more. I almost wanted to kiss him right there and then.

"I thought about you all week, Cee Jay. I came here tonight hoping you would be too. And then I start by saying something stupid like I did before."

I patted him on his brown tweed jacket shoulder. "I'm glad that I came here tonight, Tim; and I'm glad that you did too." There was a moment neither of us spoke. "Let me buy my new friend a drink," I said to him and the bartender who just then come over to our end of the bar. "I'm a martini person myself, but whatever you want, Tim, it's on me."

"I'll just have a coke, thanks," he said. "I'm driving tonight, so soda's all I can handle."

Mario the bartender went about getting the coke. "Oh, you're from out of town then," I asked.

"Yes," Tim said. I take the Holland Tunnel from New Jersey."

"Coincidence. I'm from New Jersey also."

44

Tim's reaction to learning that I was from New Jersey seemed to cause him to hesitate. "Where in New Jersey?" he rather cautiously asked.

"I was born and raised in Newark." Suddenly realizing that Tim may have been disappointed about my living in New Jersey, I added, "But now I have an apartment here in the Village for the time being."

Tim seemed relieved that I was currently living in New York.

"And I'm currently living in Elizabeth," he said emphasizing the word *currently*. He seemed to be in deep thought as he finished his coke, and I played with my second martini olive.

"Would you like to leave this bar and go some- place else?" Tim asked. I knew that this question really meant: 'Let's go to your place and have sex,' but coming from Tim, I really couldn't be sure. Perhaps he only wanted to experience a different bar and go into it feeling more comfortable with someone he knew. Perhaps he thought he could use me as a sort of gay guide to the Village. If so, he was certainly picking the wrong man. Perhaps he just wanted to go to a quieter place just to talk. Perhaps he wanted to get away from the smell of smoke, beer, and lard from the burger burner against the side wall.

I really wanted to know more about Tim Donnelly.

"How about a walk over to the Square?" I suggested.

"That sounds exactly what I may have had in mind." He emphasized the *may* and smiled.

I called Mario over to pay my tab. The bartender accepted my usual tip and nodded his head with a wink. It was as though I could read his mind saying: 'Good luck. Have fun. He seems like a catch.'

Tim and I went outside into the cool, beautiful, late October night. New York City is vibrant and exhilarating all the time, but to me early fall is the best. The leaves on the few trees can be seen in their varied shades as they gently fall. The air is clear and crisp with the aroma of burning chestnuts. The off-Broadway shows had just let out, and as we walked to Washington Square, we overheard good and bad comments about each of them. A group of ladies seemed particularly enthusiastic in their appraisal of **Man of La Mancha**, which I had seen with my friend Jack two weeks earlier.

Washington Square was filled with college kids on skate boards or throwing frizzbies. Some of the out-of-town theater types were strolling around the fountain and 'oohing' and 'aahing' over the floodlights on the arch as they played with their flash cameras to get their friends in the picture with the best angle views. As always, old men were silently playing chess on cement tables; the men seemed to be oblivious to the people who gathered around them to watch. Youngsters were playing in the fountain under the protection of their adoring parents. Tim Donnelly and I bought soft pretzels and found an empty bench.

"So," Tim began, wiping some mustard from his lips with his handkerchief, what brings a boy from Newark, New Jersey, to live in Greenwich Village?"

"Living in the Village is a short-term experience for me. After teaching in a high school, I decided to work full-time on a doctorate here at New York University. If and when I get my Ph.D., I'll return to Jersey."

"What high school did you go to?" Tim asked.

"I went to Saint Benedicts in Newark. Coincidently, one of my friends who lives in my building also graduated from there."

"I take it that you are a catholic than."

I shook and nodded my head. "Well, if by being taught by nuns for eight years and priests for four and not seeing the inside of a church in many years means your catholic, yes, I guess you can say I'm catholic."

Tim was again silent and seemingly in deep thought.

"Okay, Mr. Donnelly, I told you why I'm in New York. Now it's your turn. Why are you sneaking out of Elizabeth, on this beautiful fall Saturday evening to come to New York?"

"I told you before. I came here hoping to meet you."

"And last Saturday?"

The silence between us was now palpable. We turned to look directly at one another. Tim's eyes nearly devoured me, both with their beauty and sadness; his expression was one of pained longing.

"It's a long story, Cee Jay. It will have to wait for another time." Again there was a long pause.

"I hope that you're not disappointed in me, Tim. I mean for bringing you here rather than to my apartment."

"Yes, and no. I would like to see you again, though. Perhaps next weekend we can get to know one another better. I'll call you, if you give me your telephone number."

It had not taken me long to learn that in New York when two guys meet, don't have sex, but part exchanging telephone numbers that it is a cliché for saying 'Nice knowing you,' 'bon voyage,' 'better luck with the next guy,' 'I'm outta here.'

But I really liked Tim Donnelly and wanted to be his friend-but only a platonic friend. Perhaps if we met again I could explain this to him and he would understand. Could two men be good friends and not be homosexual? This question had plagued me since I heard it as a line in **Cat on a Hot Tin Roof.** I gave him my card with my telephone number on it; on the back I wrote "Thank you being here tonight."

When I gave him my card, he looked at it carefully, and smiled when he read the personal message on the back. As he started putting it carefully into his wallet, I asked if he was going to give me his number.

"I don't think that I can do that, Cee Jay. Perhaps some other time. Okay?"

"Ah, so Timmy is married and doesn't want his pretty little wife to get any ideas, huh!"

"Yeah, it's something like that…. marriage," Tim said. We shook hands more warmly than when we first met. Very briefly I tried to look into those beautiful eyes and caught what I believed to be a tear forming.

I sat back down on the bench as Tim Donnelly walked away from me in the direction of Fifth Avenue.

❧

When I gave Tim Donnelly my telephone number, I thought that I would not hear from him. After a few weeks I forgot about him.

I was in my apartment reading over my notes on Mark Twain for a paper I was writing on **Huckleberry Finn** as a symbol of America's transition from an agrarian to an industrial nation when the phone rang. I wondered who might be calling at 11:00 on a Wednesday evening, but welcomed the interruption from my erudite but boring task.

"Hello, is this Cee Jay?" The voice on the other end seemed soft, almost as though he were whispering.

"Yes. This is Cee Jay."

"My name is Tim Donnelly. We met at La Bar a few weeks ago. You gave me your telephone number."

Hearing this I had to collect my thoughts for a moment. "Yes, I remember you, Tim. You're from Elizabeth, New Jersey, right?"

"Sorry that it's taken me so long to get back to you. I've been…." He paused as if trying to make up an excuse or a lie. "I've been occupied," Tim said.

"That's okay," I said. "I'm glad that you didn't lose my number. How long has it been- a month or two since we met?"

"Saturday will be five weeks," Tim said.

"Well, how are you, Tim?"

"I'm okay, I guess." He hesitated before beginning again. "I'm going to be in Manhattan this Saturday. I was hoping that we could get together."

"Sure. I have no special plans for Saturday night. "I'll probably be at the bar, so, sure, I'd be glad to meet you."

"Well, I was rather hoping to meet you in the late afternoon and at your apartment, rather than the bar."

This statement caught me by surprise. Tim Donnelly was practically a stranger to me and a stranger who was – as I remembered from our meeting "five weeks ago"- rather mysterious. Other than having Paul, George, Diane, and a study group visit me once, I had not invited anyone to my apartment. His suggesting an afternoon meeting rather than at night made me curious, however. I thought about those beautiful, sad eyes that were waiting for a response from me. "What time were you thinking of?" I asked.

"Is four o'clock okay? I have to be back in Elizabeth by eleven at the latest."

My previous suspicion that Tim was married and somehow managed to create some excuse to his wife for this Saturday seemed confirmed. "Four o'clock is fine," I said. "Perhaps we can have dinner in a good Italian restaurant I know. But why don't we meet in the bar rather than my place?"

"La Bar is too loud and there are too many people. I'd like to talk to you, get to know one another better without all the distractions and the smoke."

Tim seemed determined to visit with me in my place, so after some discussion of how messy my apartment was, how small it was, etc. I gave him my address and told him that I was looking forward to meeting him again.

"The next two-and-a-half days are going to be very long for me; but until then, Cee Jay, goodbye. See you at four on Saturday."

It was too late and I was too preoccupied with my thoughts of Tim Donnelly to return to Huck Finn and the concept of my premise that night. I forced myself to complete the paper on Thursday and Friday. I was thinking too much of Tim Donnelly. Was this a "date" I had with him? My first "gay" date? I was nervous and confused. On Saturday morning I dusted, washed the pile of dishes in the sink, and organized books and records, etc. I was giddy with anticipation.

As four o'clock approached I began to doubt whether Tim would show up. I made a martini to calm down. I kept thinking that Tim was 'just another flake, like all the other gay men in the world.' At 4:15 I went to the bathroom. I then made another martini. 'Yes,' I thought, *He's just another flake. I might as well get used to it.*

At 4:25 I was positive that he had stood me up. I was just about to swallow the last drop of my martini, when the buzzer sounded. My heart beat faster as I pressed the button. *Maybe he wasn't a flake, or worse yet, a figment of my imagination. He really did come to visit me!'*

"Hello, It's Tim."

"Hi, Tim. I'll buzz you in, but be prepared. I'm on the fourth floor and there are no elevators."

"Good thing I'm in good shape then. I'll run up those stairs," Tim said jovially.

As soon as I buzzed him in, I ran into the bathroom to gargle with mouthwash to cover any hint of gin on my breath.

Indeed, he must have run up the stairs because no sooner had I put the empty martini glass in the kitchen cabinet, when I heard him knocking on the front door.

"Sorry I'm so late," Tim said as soon as I opened the door. "I had a hard time finding a parking space." He handed me a bottle of red wine. "I could use a glass of this right now. Traffic getting through the tunnel was horrendous." After giving me the wine, he hesitated before shaking my hand. "I'm also a little bit nervous. You know, about coming here."

"Well, I'm glad you're here. And to tell the truth, I'm a little bit nervous also."

He smiled warmly. Tim was even better looking than I remembered him. He was approximately my height of 6'2," had a head of thick, brown hair that seemed lighter than I first noted, and he seemed tanner. He was wearing a white polo shirt which seemed to emphasize his muscular body. He wore tight fitting jeans, which drew my attention to his crotch and well-rounded butt. But his one feature that I remembered so well was his beautiful light blue eyes. They spoke of boyishness, of innocence.

"I'll open the wine right now," I said as I turned to go into the kitchen. "Just make yourself comfortable."

"Do you mind if I follow you?" Tim asked.

"Not at all. I'll show you around my humble abode. I'm afraid there isn't much to see, however."

"I see you made your bed," Tim said upon entering the bedroom. "I'm impressed."

"And this is my very own culinary fantasy," I added as I went straight into the kitchen, deliberately getting out of the bedroom as soon as possible.

"mmm. Will I experience your culinary prowess today or are we going out for dinner?"

"I really hadn't even thought of it, so I guess we can go out later, if you'd like." I reached for two glasses that I thought best resembled wine glasses.

"That's fine with me," Tim obliged. "Perhaps some time we can cook together. I'm a pretty good chef, if I must say so."

"Oh, did you graduate from the Culinary Institute or something?" I said.

Tim laughed. "Nothing like that! But my Irish mother made sure her only son knew how to cook. She taught my two sisters and me how to cook. They are both married now, and when I visit them I do the cooking because they say that I am better in the kitchen than they are. I do enjoy cooking though."

"I'll have to remember that," I said as I gave him a half full tumbler of wine. We touched glasses. "Here's to us," I said as a toast. "Shall we retire to the drawing room?" I jokingly said as I led him back into the living room via the bedroom.

Again, he paused for a moment in the bedroom. "How long are you going to stay here?"

"In June I signed a year's lease, but since I moved in I've met some friends who live in the building and we've become rather close. I like it here. It's convenient to the university, so I might renew my lease and stay here until I get my degree."

Back in the living room we sat together on the futon. If he were thinking of my rather Spartan furnishings, he did not mention them. He seemed more interested in talking about the courses I was taking and what my dissertation would be on. After a while he got up to explore my limited record collection. I knelt beside him on the floor.

"You obviously like show music, classical, and a little pop," Tim said as he shuffled through my limited collection of 33and1/3 rds.

"Yes. What would you like to hear?"

"I like show music also, but generally prefer classical to pop…. How about playing this one?" Tim handed me the original cast album of ***West Side Story***.

53

"Good choice!" I said. "I loved the play when I saw it and have been wearing out the recording."

We returned to the futon when the record started. We remained silent during the overture and the first few numbers. Perhaps it was the two martinis and now the wine which gave me enough courage to move closer to Tim and put my arm over his shoulder. When I did this, he turned and gave a smile. He grabbed my hand and held it firmly.

During the song "There's a Place For Us" we turned to look at one another. I saw those beautiful eyes. I knew I had to have him. I desired to move my fingers across his face, to rub my fingers through his hair, to feel the warmth of his lips against mine. Our noses dabbed. We began to kiss. I closed my eyes... Yes, yes. ...This is the one. We both pulled back. We gazed momentarily at one another. I gently caressed his eyes with my lips. He touched my chin. I forced him down on the futon. I ravished his mouth with my kisses. Our tongues intertwined. I pulled back. We smiled. I fingered the corner of his lips. He grabbed my head and pulled me into him. I sat up. I started to pull on his polo shirt. He obliged by sitting up; I removed his shirt and began kissing his chest. I gently nibbled on his tits. I bit the small hairs around one tit before moving to the other. He fell into my shoulders. I lifted him gently to the floor.

"Let's go mess up that nicely made bed," I said. He turned toward the bedroom. I put both arms around his bare chest. We were both standing aside the bed. I reached for his belt and undid the bucket. I lovingly forced him onto the bed. I lay on top of him. We began to kiss. We both turned sideways. Locked in this embrace we turned again so that now he was on top of me. He began to unbutton my shirt. As he did, I reached out to his crotch. I felt that he was erect.

"mmm…" he said.

"mmm, indeed!" I said as I unzipped his fly and pulled his pants down as far as possible. I felt his firm cock though his white jockey shorts.

Tim got off the bed. He quickly removed his shoes and pants, but kept his socks and underwear on. He went to the front of the bed and removed my shoes. "Undo that buckle," he softly commanded. When I did he began pulling my pants off. I lifted my butt to make the pull on my pants less strenuous. Tim fell onto me again. We writhed in the pleasure of rubbing our bodies together while we kissed. I turned him over; I wanted to see that beautiful rounded ass. I had desired to touch it the moment he walked in. Now covered only by his briefs, it was more tempting to me. I gently spread his legs and reached under to grab the front of his shorts. With his underwear down to his knees, I turned him over. I took off my own briefs and got next to him. We kissed passionately. I put his cock in my hands. He did the same. We then embraced one another with both hands. The sensation of our two cocks touching one another was incredible. I noticed that the slightest movement on my part caused his penis to react as if in a jump. I thought how wonderful it was to have this man so close. I slid down on the bed and reached for his cock with my mouth. He moaned with pleasure. I ran his manhood in and out of my mouth while creating pressure on it. The tip of my tongue found his slit and I played around it. Tim began to twitch as though he would momentarily have an ejaculation. I removed my mouth and began to slide back up to him.

"Oh, God! You have no idea how crazy that makes me."

"You like that, huh," I said.

"Oh, yes!" He smiled sheepishly.

"Guess, what, Timmy…. I love sucking your beautiful, big cock."

Tim leaned into me and we kissed again. "Do you want me to do that to you?" he softly asked.

"Sure, if you want to."

"I've never done it before," Tim admitted.

This revelation startled me. He seemed so forward, so aggressive that hearing him admit that he had never sucked a guy's dick before was bewildering. I wondered if I were the first man he ever had sex with. *Surely*, I thought, *he can't be a virgin to gay sex*…. yet… I didn't know quite how to react. I pushed him down. "Try it, you might like it" was all I could think of saying.

He did readily try it, but I felt that he really wasn't into it. I don't know if it was his newness to the act or the mental state which his admission put me into, but he didn't excite me. It felt that he was deliberately performing fellatio to satisfy me, rather than both of us. Yet he had said that it made him "crazy" when I sucked him. Was he terribly passive in his love making? He got it from others- perhaps his wife- but never reciprocated. I reached down and began playing his ass. Perhaps he wanted to be fucked. I certainly wanted to fuck him. I wanted to get inside him. Here was a man I truly liked, and this would have been the most masculine of human activities; the thought of the two of us thus engaged was pleasure unto itself.

My attempts to suggest fucking by playing with his butt didn't seem to be going any- where so I turned him over on his stomach. I rubbed my cock on his ass. I inserted a finger into his butt hole and wiggled it around. He became somewhat rigid, so I was forced to ask. "Do you want me to fuck you, Tim?"

"No, not today. I'm sorry. Perhaps some other time."

As much as I wanted to get my dick inside those big, round checks of his, I wasn't about to rape him or frighten him. I lay next to him again and looked into those beautiful eyes of his. Perhaps he really was a virgin, a complete innocent. I kissed him.

"I'm sorry," Tim said. "I'm kind of new at this. Let's take it slow. Okay? I hope I'm not a disappointment to you today."

I kissed him again and he reacted positively by grabbing my cock.

We continued to kiss and caress and jerk one another for several more minutes. But for me, when we did both climax it was more like mutual masturbation than love. I got up and went to the bathroom to wash myself off. I returned with a wet cloth and towel to wipe him off.

We both got dressed and had another glass of wine before I suggested that we go out for dinner. To my surprise, he agreed to go. I rather thought that he might be ready to head home to New Jersey; I had lost some of my passion for him when I realized that he was not a thrilling sex partner as I would have desired. But he was handsome and genuinely seemed like a nice guy. I was also curious about him. I had some unanswered questions: Was he really gay? Was his married life on the rocks? Was he even married? Was this his first sexual encounter- gay or straight? I was intrigued enough to want to spend a bit more time with him. Perhaps over dinner I would get some answers.

We went to a small, family-style Italian restaurant that I knew of that was in the neighborhood. I had been there before with a group from NYU, and it seemed "neutral enough" for this occasion. Many of the restaurants in the Village that had a gay cliental were noisy, filled with smoke, had tables practically one atop the other, and over-priced.

At least here at Luigi's, two men without female companions were not treated as alien invaders as was usual in most non-gay establishments. The term "gay friendly" was still a few years in the making. In the 1960's everything seemed to be either "gay" or "straight." This included bars, restaurants, and even churches.

We were led to a table for two in a far corner of Luigi's. The table had a red and white checkered plastic tablecloth and a votive style candle, which the waiter lit after giving us menus. Tim scanned the restaurant and seemed pleased with the general ambiance.

It was nice sitting across from this clean-cut, masculine looking and sounding man. I was glad to know him even if the gnawing feeling that we were not completely compatible in the bedroom was eating me. Tim was in many ways, except for the sex, my type.

I knew what I was going to order, so as Tim discovered the menu, I was looking at him. A thought came into my mind: I pictured two heterosexuals meeting, being physically attracted to one another, getting to know one another well, perhaps falling in love and eventually marrying. And then on the honeymoon realizing that they were not sexually compatible. Could all the platonic attractions keep such a couple faithful until death would they part? 'Virginity before marriage,' I thought, 'is fine if you live in a vacuum.'

Tim looked up at me and said, "Everything looks good here. What would you recommend?"

I saw his beautiful eyes, his beautiful hair, his handsome tanned face, his strong shoulders. I thought of that well-sculptured body, that big exciting dick, that cute small rounded ass. ...His innocence!... Even now, in the restaurant, he was asking me to lead the way rather than being an active participant in the simple task of choosing a meal.

Well, I'm having the pasta and meatballs with the house salad. It's good; I've had it here before. Their specialty is the shrimp marinara; friends tell me it's excellent."

The waiter came and we both ordered the same thing.

"Would you gentlemen like chianti with your meal?" The waiter asked.

Tim looked to me for the response. "Yes, your house magnum will be fine," I said.

The waiter quickly brought the wine, breadsticks, and our salads.

"I'm very glad I've met you, Cee Jay," Tim said as I poured the wine. "I hope that we can become special friends."

I smiled as I pondered his statement of 'special friends.' "Here's to us then," I said as we touched glasses in a toast.

Tim opened his napkin and placed it over his lap. I noticed that he then closed his eyes and lowered his head as if saying a silent grace before turning his fork into the salad. Saying grace before meals was a tradition which I had given up many years ago and which would probably be considered antediluvian in the Village, particularly among the non-Baptist gays. It did, however, add a bit of charm to this man, I thought. He did it without any flair or oral recognition; he did it without even asking me to hold his hand.

I wanted him to talk about himself. I was hoping that during our meal he would clear up some of the questions I had concerning him. I felt awkward in probing him and preferred for him to offer the answers on his own. Instead of talking about himself, however, he diverted the conversation by talking about the theater. He told me that he had always been interested in the theater and would attend it more often if he lived in the City. "Perhaps we can get to see a few plays together," he said.

I merely nodded as if to say 'That would be nice. Go on.'

I did learn that Tim preferred musicals and comedies. He said that he did very much like Jean Anouilh's **Becket,** however. He considered Tennessee Williams to be a great playwright, but one whose best writing was past.

When he said that he was intrigued by Albee's **Whose Afraid of Virginia Woolf,** I asked "How so?" This led to a lengthy discussion of Existentialism and the theater of the absurd. This topic accounted for most of the time we were eating. I found conversation with Tim stimulating and was pleasantly surprised how intelligent he seemed without being a bit pretentious. I still did not know much about his private life, however.

While waiting for the waiter to return with our check, I said, "Tim, you seem to know a lot about the theater and literature. Did you study it in college?"

Tim smiled. "No, far from it actually. But I have kept up with it in the Sunday **Times**." He paused for a moment. "I have volunteered to direct a play at a local high school, though. Don't laugh, Cee Jay, but I'm currently directing **Arsenic and Old Lace**. It's the senior class play. I think the kids are much better actors than I am a director, but it's fun working with them."

I wanted to pursue this bit of information from him, but just then the waiter arrived with our check so the conversation had to be postponed.

As we walked down Eighth Avenue, I noticed that Tim looked at his watch. As I was about to ask him the time, he offered that it was 8:30.

"Cee Jay, I don't have to be back in New Jersey for a couple of hours, so if you would be willing, I would like to go back to your apartment for a while."

"Sure." I thought of the possibility of 'round two.' *Would we have sex again*, I wondered. *Would it be better?*

Tim must have read my mind because he quickly said, "Not to have sex again. There is something you should know about me that if we are to become truly friends- as I hope we will- you need to know. I need to be fair and honest with you."

"Of course," I said aloud, but I was thinking: *Wow! Now he's going to tell me about his wife and kids back in New Jersey- or whatever else he has to hide.*

"I'm a priest."

Tim Donnelly was sitting in my living room on 10th Street. He was trying to tell me something important, something about what I needed to know if we were to continue to be friends. I fully expected him to tell me that he was married or something equally understandable. But I was totally unprepared for these three words: 'I'm a priest.'

In the early 1960's, coming from I guy that I had sex with just a few hours ago, such a statement was shocking to me. Even though many of my high school teachers were priests and throughout high school I was a devout Catholic, I never knew a priest personally. They were there, but I never gave much thought to them as human beings. They were symbols of religious authority, or objects to be admired and respected, not actual people one could pal around with. Even past age twenty-one, to me a priest was merely a man who said mass and gave a sermon. I never bothered to equate such a human behavior as sex with a priest. I just accepted the fact that they never married; perhaps I had been brainwashed into believing that they were all spotless virgins like the Blessed Mother. That they were 'men of God,' and, therefore, I thought- in my naivety- above sex. There were a few that I liked but never thought of them as being physically attractive. Now I had met one who was not only physically attractive to me but one who was personable, charming, sincere, and genuinely fun to be with. Earlier I thought that if only the love-making or sex could improve, he might become a lover, a partner- something like George and Paul downstairs.

I shook my head in confusion. "What?"

"I just told you that I'm a priest, a Roman Catholic priest," Tim said softly but with conviction.

"Why? Why are you telling me this?"

"Because I thought you would understand. Because I like you very much and want you as a special friend. And if we are to be good friends you needed to- deserved to- know this about me. I didn't want to lie to you or make up stories. I know that you were wondering about my background."

"I thought you were married," I said.

Tim smiled. "Well, perhaps in a way I am married. To Holy Mother the Church, that is."

"But priests aren't supposed to have sex. Don't you take an oath or something?"

"Yes, it's one of three oaths we take at ordination. But many people- particularly Catholics, believe it or not- confuse the word *celibacy* with *chastity*. *Celibacy* means that I can never marry. *Chastity* is a virtue which priests as well as all people should strive for; but after all, we are all humans and God does recognize our weaknesses.

"Celibacy is unique to the Catholic Church; it's one of those things that make us special. Even if I wanted to marry- which I don't, I took a sacred vow not to. I would have to leave the church, if I married, and I love the Church too much to ever leave it. That's something you must understand about me, Cee Jay. Above all else, I love being a priest. It's who I am, who I always wanted to be, and with God's help, who I always will be.

"Celibacy was first mentioned by the Apostle Paul. It became part of the Roman Canon at the Council of Elvira in 306 and has been in effect and often debated ever since. Various

Councils referred to abstaining from wives and concubines and having no children, but there was never mention of homosexual couplings in connection with marriage."

"Isn't the Second Vatican Council supposed to end that archaic vow which doesn't permit priests to marry?" I asked.

"No, that idea has been kicked around since the days of Martin Luther, but the Council never took any of those rumors seriously. The best that may come out of the Council is to permit men to become priests who were married before they are ordained. Converts and widowers, for example. Sometimes I feel sorry for my Episcopalian counter parts whose wives wish they weren't married. People don't realize how difficult it must be to have a wife and family and be a religious leader and model at the same time. It's very time consuming and you have to be fully devoted to what you are doing. You can't be a good team player, if your loyalties are divided between teams."

"Yes," I said, "but what about homosexuality? The Church condemns it, doesn't it?"

"I really don't want to and can't speak for Rome," Tim began. "But for me personally, I believe that God created all men in His image. He created me with the desire to be attracted to men, as He has many millions of men and women throughout human history. I look at being homosexual as a gift from God with a purpose. Perhaps that very purpose is to be a priest. Oh, I try to channel my desires, I pray to avoid temptation; but I am human. I would have been here four weeks ago, but I was asked to coach our elementary school basketball team at my church. Then the high school kids asked me to direct their class play. For me, these things come first. I may never have kids of my own, but I love working with kids. I give of myself more than I possibly could if they were my own or if I had a wife and house to take care of. Being a priest IS my job, just as any married man has a job and must care for his own."

"Damn it, Tim, don't get off the subject here! You're gay, right? You preach against it. Doesn't the church consider it a sin? But here you are fucking around with me! Isn't that just a little bit hypocritical?

Tim bowed his head and thought for a moment before responding. "Yes, perhaps it is in a way." There was a long pause before he continued. "I knew that I wanted to be a priest from the time I was in grammar school. I was an altar boy and loved being in church and serving the priests at mass, I loved the ritual, I loved the music, I loved the smell of incense. It wasn't until I was in an all-boy catholic high school that I began to think of other boys in a physical sense. I couldn't erase that desire any more than I could erase the desire to become a priest.

"I went into the minor seminary at Seton Hall University right from high school. It was there that I learned that I wasn't the only one with conflicting desires. Actually, it was there that I learned about being gay. You know, Kinsey told us that between six and ten percent of all men are homosexual. I discovered that among seminarians that figure is more like 50%. True many are weeded out by the time that they get into Darlington, our major seminary; but the figure, as far as I could determine, was still about 25 to 35 percent.

"The Church knows this and tells us to pray and fight against it. During their six years of study and prayer many know they can't stand being around only men and enjoy the company of a man-only society without succumbing to the physical pleasures of sex, so they drop out. My spiritual adviser and confessor told me to keep enduring and if necessary to develop a special friend- that's what he called it- "a special friend" with whom to have sex while mutually loving God more than one another. This worked for me, Cee Jay, and 'my special friend.' Of the twelve of us who were ordained that year, six of us were homosexual from birth." Tim thought about what he just said and snickered. "The bishop made sure we were all sent to different parishes, but we still keep in touch.

"I guess it's easier for a monastic priest or monk to remain chaste. The guys like me- sectarians and the Jesuits- find it more difficult. We have to live in the real world and work among families and youngsters. We have to fight temptation constantly. Jesuits tell me that teaching in a college and being surrounded by young men is really tough on them. That's why some of us leave the priesthood. Others turn to alcohol. Some straight guys occasionally visit prostitutes or literally keep mistresses. But all of us- whether we are hetero or homo- want to keep the vow of celibacy."

I listened carefully to all that Tim was telling me. I was impressed by his sincerity. I had never given these things much interest before, and this new perspective into Catholicism was enlightening. At the bar I had recently heard disparaging and unsubstantiated rumors about the Roman hierarchy. One particularly nasty rumor concerned the cardinal and his entertaining so-called "altar boys" on his yacht in the East River.

It was getting late. I also was getting annoyed with Tim. Earlier I had thought of him as a potential lover, but now I looked at him as someone with whom I could not possibly develop the kind of relationship that George and Paul had. Theirs was the relationship which I sought.

The landlord had not yet turned on the heat in the building, and the living room window was open for fresh air, but now I felt chilly. I got up and closed the window. I also needed a moment's pause in this conversation, which by now I found to be frustrating.

Sitting back down, I asked the question which made me angry even to think of it, but I felt compelled to ask: "Do you think that what we did in the bedroom a few hours ago was a sin?"

Tim thought carefully about his response before beginning. "The answer to that question cannot really be simplified to a yes or no. I consider sin as a deliberate act against the laws of God and nature. The laws of God, however, are told by men interpreting nature. I believe- and I have to emphasize that it is only my belief- I believe that sin is a little like beauty. It's in the eye of the beholder; therefore, if you feel you commit a sin, you probably have.

"Much of our Christian-Judaic beliefs find their source in the Bible. As you know, we Catholics don't put as much emphasis on the Bible, except, perhaps, for the four gospels and Psalms. Much of the uproar today about homosexuality stems from the Old Testament, particularly "Leviticus." A single sentence from "Leviticus" is the basis which many Christians say makes it a sin. What these people fail to realize is that most of "Leviticus" is outdated and in many cases silly. Taken out of the context in which it was written "Leviticus" would permit slavery, the banning of women during their menstrual cycles, the banning of eating of shellfish and pork. It also would ban anyone who is deformed, lame, or retarded.

"I prefer a passage from Romans 14, in which Paul wrote- and this one I have memorized- 'I know, and am persuaded by the Lord Jesus, that there is nothing unclean of itself; but to him that esteemeth anything to be unclean, to him it is unclean.' Paul also said in Romans 13:' Love your neighbor as yourself. Love does no harm to its neighbor. Therefore love is the fulfillment of the law.'

"You know," Tim continued, "some churches are carefully studying the whole moral and spiritual aspects of sin and homosexuality. The Bishop of the Episcopal Dioceses of Newark, for example, has just written a book on the subject. He titled it **None Dare Call It Sin**. It's an excellent study on the subject. I'll give you my copy, next time we get together."

He looked at his watch. "It's getting late. I better be going. I have a 7:30 mass tomorrow, and my pastor gets excited when any of us stay out past midnight."

We both got up and went to the door. Before I could open it, Tim extended his hand which I did take but while shaking hands I reached around him with my other hand and gave him a tight hug.

As I put our checks together, he said, "I'm really glad I came here today. I'll call you, so we can get together again soon."

Then he said something which really blew my mind. "By the way, my name isn't Tim Donnelly."

I closed and locked the door behind him. I stood for moment, reviewing the whole experience of his visit. I shook my head and said aloud: "Damn hypocrite!"

Chapter Six

FAT FREDDY FUSCETTI

I met Fat Freddy on Friday, February 22. It was his birthday. He was thirty- six. Freddy didn't walk into La Bar. He seemed to have sailed in on a cloud. A thunder cloud of laughter. He was surrounded by a retinue of fluffy clouds from which barbs shot like bolts of lightning, followed by uproarious laughter. Amidst it all was a short, plump, balding man who was beaming like a ray of sunshine peeking through the heavy layers of smoke that always seemed to penetrate the atmosphere of the bar. He wore a burly white, faux fur. Wrapped around his neck and hanging down to his waist was a bright green satin scarf. This center of attention resembled a snowman more than any human. Freddy was waving his hands as though he were drying finger nail polish. Occasionally he would point to one of his cohorts, and say something that caused more laughter. It was indeed a festive, "gay" crowd. But I guess that's why I liked going to La Bar. You never knew who or what may come through the doors.

It didn't take long to learn that this was his birthday. Once the companions had gotten their drinks, they gathered around him, and with glasses raised began singing "Happy Birthday."

When they finished with the traditional "Happy Birthday, Dear Freddy," everyone in the place, including myself, started to clap. A flashbulb went off. almost immediately as the clapping subsided, one of the regulars at the bar yelled, "How old are you?" There was a moment of embarrassing silence as those in Freddy's circle seemed shocked by the anathema. Even Freddy seemed stunned by the question.

"Darling, boy, if you must know, I am thirty-six. Next year I shall be thirty-five and, like you, I shall remain thirty-five forever." Another flash bulb illuminated the event.

Everyone, including the man who asked the question, broke out in laughter. As an encore to his retort, Freddy threw his green satin scarf up in a flutter over his shoulder. I could almost guess his thinking: *Take that, you peasant!*

Myself and everyone else went on with our own conversations or cruising. Freddy and company seemed to settle down into their own revelry.

"Well, hello there, handsome. Where have you been all my thirty-five years?"

Turning, I saw that non-other than birthday boy Freddy was standing next to me at the bar. I didn't know if he were attempting to replenish his drink or introduce himself to me. "Hello," I stammered in surprise. "Ah, congratulations and happy birthday."

"Thank, you, thank you, thank you, dear boy." He extended his limp hand for a soft handshake. "I'm Freddy, Freddy Fuscetti. And to whom do I owe the pleasure?"

"Everyone just calls me Cee Jay."

"Everyone calls me Freddy, but my given name is Fredrich, but only my mama calls me Fredrich. I do wish people would call me Fred, but alas, I'm stuck with Freddy."

At that moment, the bar tender appeared in front of us. Taking our empty glasses, he asked if we were ready for refills.

"Er, yes. Freddy, what are you drinking. Since today is your birthday, let me buy you a drink?" Almost immediately I was sorry I offered to buy him a drink because this would mean he may stay next to me longer than I really would appreciate, which would have been about ten seconds.

"Why, thank you very much, dear boy!" Freddy didn't speak. He gushed. "I would like a black Russian, if you please, sir. On the rocks."

The bartender walked away to make Freddy's drink and my second martini.

"I do like to drink black Russians," Freddy said. He smiled at me. "But tonight I would prefer a big, white Russian, to play with. If you get my drift, Mr. Cee Jay."

"I do," I said.

"Is this your regular haunt?"

"I guess you can say so. I live around the corner, and when I go out for a drink, it is always here. I've only lived in the Village a few months, and haven't been to any other bar."

"Really!" Freddy seemed surprised. "Dear boy, we must show you to other habitations in this wonderful city. This place is acceptable, I suppose, if you are in the mood for the types that frequent this establishment; but really, darling, you should set higher standards."

I felt like socking the pompous fairy, but retorted with a barb of my own. "Freddy why do you refer to me and others as 'dear boy'? It sounds like a British affectation, but I don't think you are from the UK."

"Oh, it must be an 'affectation,' as you say, that I picked up when my sister and I lived in merry old England. You see, Cee Jay, I am a bit of an anglophile." Our drinks were delivered. "Well, I must be getting back to my chums. Perhaps, I shall see you later Mr. Cee Jay."

I fully expected to see him throw the other end of his scarf over his shoulder as he turned away.

"An interesting man, that one," the man sitting next to me said, in what clearly was a British accent. "One day he was in here and after taking to him a while, I discovered that when he says he lived in England, he was referring to a two-week holiday tour with his sister and a bus load of other Yanks."

I laughed. "Yeah, I thought it was something like that."

I would have liked to continue talking to this man, but he shortly finished his drink and left saying, "Cheerio. See you about."

Minutes later I finished my drink and was about to leave the bar when I was joined once again by Freddy.

"I say old chap, my chums and I are about to depart this bar and head to a place uptown. It's a piano bar and they play live music, not that noise that comes from the jukebox.

I would be much honored if you joined us."

I glanced over at his 'chums' who were all looking in my direction. For the most part, they all looked like attractive, decent guys even if they did seem a bit effeminate. One man, whom I guessed might be in his early thirties, was dressed in a black tuxedo. He was also the best-looking member of the coterie. The night was still young, I didn't have any classes the next day, and I had no desire to go back to my lonely apartment. Perhaps it was the effect of two martinis that loosened me enough to accept Freddy's invitation for a new adventure in the big city.

Before leaving La bar, Freddy introduced me to his friends. I shook hands with each of them, particularly noticing how warm and gentle the man wearing the tuxedo was. Freddy arranged that he and I and the tuxedoed man, Larry, would ride in one cab and the other three men would follow in another cab. We walked the short distance to Sixth Avenue to hail our cabs.

On the way uptown, I asked Larry if he were wearing a tuxedo to celebrate Freddy's birthday. He explained that he was a violinist and had played at Carnegie Hall earlier and did not have a change of clothes. He also told me that he lived in New Jersey and that his full-time position was teaching music in a high school there. I got the impression that if nothing else would be gained from meeting Freddy, at least Larry and I could become friends… or more. At this point in my life, I was often thinking of the 'more.'

The cab let us out in front of a nondescript building in the west 50's. There was no sign or other indication that the building contained a gay bar. Freddy had told me before we arrived that the management would provide me with a tie and jacket. In order to be admitted into the bar one had to be properly attired, he informed me. "A certain organization which owns this establishment tries to keep the riffraff that is welcome in La Bar away from this residential neighborhood. New York's law officers think it is a gentlemen's club, you know."

Inside the lobby, we were greeted by a hat/coat check man who was nattily attired in a double-breasted suit with vest and tie. Freddy addressed him as Axel and Axel, in turn, smiled and said, "Good evening, Mr. Fuscetti. I see your friend will need a tie and jacket." To me he cheerfully asked, "Will blue serge with a red, stripped tie be acceptable tonight, sir?"

Upon entering the main room, I was immediately surprised by the large, crystal chandelier which hung from the ceiling of the two-story room. A sweeping, semi-circular staircase leading to the second floor gave the room a grand and elegant appearance. Freddy led his entourage to the bar on one side of the room. None of us sang "Happy Birthday" and Freddy didn't tell any obscene jokes to loud laughter. Generally, the room was subdued with a few of the men smoking and having quiet conversations.

"Come, gentlemen," Freddy said, "we must show Cee Jay the rest of the establishment."

From the bar area, he directed us down a small hall. Rest rooms were on both sides. The hall opened to a room which was about three times larger than the main room we had just been in. Along the carpeted edges of this room were small tables. Each table had just two chairs. The only light in the room came from votive candles on each table and a small spot on the live trio playing in the far corner. I realized I was indeed having an adventure when I saw six couples- all male- slow dancing on the wooden dance floor. The idea of men dancing together in such an intimate, night club atmosphere had never entered my imagination. I wondered if George and Paul had ever been here. I also pictured my coming back here sometime with Larry.

"Quite different from La Bar, wouldn't you saw, Cee Jay," Freddy said with a smile. "Should the need arise, Axel will alert the dancers by pressing a button that will flash blinking red lights in the ceiling. Come. We must see who is at the piano upstairs this evening. Perhaps I shall sing for you gentlemen this evening."

When we got to the top of the carpeted grand staircase, Freddy moved aside to indicate that we should all go to the side and look down over the rail to observe the room from which we just ascended. "From here one may observe all the pretty, young boys before they are gobbled up by the other vultures like us," Freddy pronounced.

I noted that there were restrooms behind us on this level. Bright brass plates indicated your choice of 'Mesdames' or 'Messieurs'. *How tres piss elegant,* I thought as I followed Freddy into the grand saloon.

The room was approximately as large as the dance room on the first floor. This room, however, was fully carpeted. There were larger round tables with four chairs throughout the center of the room. Smaller tables with two chairs were along the walls. A baby grand piano occupied a small raised platform in one corner. The performer was attired in a black tuxedo with tails. Freddy directed us to a table near the performer, indicating that Larry and I should sit at his table with Ben, while Jonathan and a thin man, whose name also was Fred, would sit together at an adjoining table. I had thought that these two may have been lovers while the four of us were 'unattached.' To distinguish between the two Freds in our party, I mentally attached the appellations 'Fat Freddy' and 'skinny Freddy.'

The pianist was playing and singing what appeared to be a somewhat bawdy tune which had a refrain of "But don't tell momma." The other men who were scattered throughout the room seemed to be enjoying it, and there was some mild laughter. I took note of the fact that the entertainer did smile and lower his face in recognition of Freddy.

Almost immediately, a waiter was at our table. He quickly took the red 'Reserved' tag from our table. "Good evening, Mr. Fuscetti. I hope you are having a pleasant birthday." He looked at our group, smiled, and said, "Gentlemen, welcome. My name is Donald." I thought that Donald was very handsome, probably a would-be actor waiting on tables and/or hustling here in the evenings, hoping to meet 'the right people,' while going for auditions during the day. He looked to be about my age. He wore black pants, a white shirt, with a black and silver paisley vest and a red bow tie. "I will be right back with your champagne." As he departed I noticed his very firm, bubble-butt ass.

I looked at Larry, who must have seen the expression on my face. "Freddy made reservations here, Cee Jay," he said.

A door to the left of the piano platform opened and Donald and another waiter fitting the stereotype entered pushing a cart with glasses and an ice bucket with a magnum of champagne. There also were two trays of assorted cheeses and crackers for each of our tables.

The cart pusher placed the flutes in front of each of us as well as the pianist, while Donald pored the bubbly.

As the last glass was being filled, the pianist stopped playing to make an announcement. "Gentlemen, we are particularly happy to welcome a special guest tonight, Mr. Freddy Fuscetti, who is here to celebrate his birthday with us." He led the room in singing "Happy Birthday, Dear Freddy." With the last refrain, he lifted his glass toward Freddy, as we all did before taking a sip of the champagne. As we clapped, Jonathan had his camera set to take pictures Then, as if on cue, the service door opened again and another cart was rolled in with a large cake and plastic dishes, forks, and a large silver knife and server. I took note that no one asked how old Freddy was in this atmosphere and the cake had only one large candle burning brightly.

Ceremoniously, Freddy closed his eyes for a moment as though he were making a wish- *probably for the biggest white Russian imaginable,* I thought- before blowing out the candle. Again, the bulb of Jonathan's camera flashed. Again, the room exploded in clapping. Another flash caught Freddy cutting the first piece of the cake which he also ceremoniously presented to Ben, who blew him a kiss. The second piece went to Larry and I was given the third piece. Donald then took over the cutting and his assistant delivered cake to Jonathan and Stewart's table. The last piece Donald cut was intended for Freddy.

As we ate our cake, the pianist continued to play and sing "Times, They are a Changing."

The cart waiter began to circle the room to offer cake to any gentleman who wanted a piece. Donald refilled each of our champagne flutes.

The piano player finished his routine song. "Gentlemen," he said into the microphone. "Let's give a hand of applause to encourage our birthday celebrant, Mr. Freddy Fuscetti to come up and sing for us." His own clapping was followed by everyone at the two tables and then by everyone else in the room.

It really did not take much encouragement for Freddy to go up to the pianist, exchange a few words of what was to be played, and take the microphone.

"Thank you, gentlemen, thank you for your kind encouragement," Freddy said. "But really, I do so enjoy singing here. You know it is my joy to perform before you whenever I can. So, maestro, if you please, *Santa Lucia.*"

Freddy did have a rich tenor voice and sang very beautifully. His ease and the way he stood next to the grand piano gave me the impression that he may have been a trained, operatic singer. He seemed almost carried away by the music and the words which he sang in Italian. I thought that he actually would start to cry on "O dolce Napoli, o suol beato."

Jonathan got a picture of Freddy basking in the applause that followed "Santa Lucia."

"Thank you, gentlemen. Now, from the land of my forefathers, to a place which we are all much closer to, the west side of Manhattan, I would like to sing for you "There's a Place for Us" from **West Side Story.** As Freddy sang this beautiful song, I could sense that he was singing these sad words to all homosexuals, because the song had double meaning to the gay community. I saw that several members of the audience, including Larry, were crying. I myself fought back tearing.

When he finished, there was no applause. Emotion was too raw. Many including myself were too moved. It was a moment which I knew I should never forget. Instead of clapping, the audience was yelling "Encore! Encore!"

"Do you want me to sing one more for you?" Freddy asked his audience. "Let's see, what shall I sing for you?" He paused in thought. "I know. I shall ask my new friend, whom I have brought here tonight for his first time, Mr. Cee Jay, to select a number for us." I was startled that Freddy had introduced me in this way. I was speechless. "Come on, Cee Jay, tell us what you would like me to sing for you and this wonderful assemblage of friends."

The week before I had seen a new play in the Village called **Man of La Mancha** and was particularly moved by some of the songs in it. For a moment I could picture Freddy, with fine tenor voice, being in this play. Almost instinctively, I called out "The Impossible Dream."

"Ah, an excellent choice!" Freddy gushed. "I see someone has been to the ANTA Washington Square Theatre recently." He turned to the piano player, who indicated that he did know the music by ear and could play it in Freddy's pitch.

As I listened in awe as Freddy sang, I knew that I was experiencing an epiphany. I knew that I was right in choosing to work for a doctorate in the most vibrant and exciting city in the world. The sacrifices I was making in order to do so were fulfilling my own 'impossible dream.' I was also glad in having chosen to 'go with the flow' by meeting and accompanying this unusual man who was expanding my horizons in accepting people. At this time and place I had opened myself to all of life's adventures. I knew that I would not continue to shut doors.

As the merriment continued in the main salon, as nature dictated, I excused myself to visit the restroom. Even going to the bathroom in this gentlemen's club was different. The 'messieurs' room was bright, even though most of it was black, polished marble. Unlike the one urinal at La Bar, this place had four and there were partitions separating each. There were also three separate toilet stalls, to La Bar's one. The air was constantly filtered, thus blocking all unpleasant odors. I took particular notice of the restroom attendant who was standing by with a hand towel as soon as a patron finished at one of the three sinks. I thought about the fact that more often than not, the paper towel dispenser at La Bar was empty.

Before the evening ended, Freddy and I exchanged telephone numbers on the back of match book covers found on all the tables and bars. Even the match books in this place were elegant with a satin black finish with silver lettering. Larry and I also exchanged telephone numbers using the pre-printed 'name' and 'number' spaces on the match books.

Freddy, Larry, and I shared a cab. Larry had left his car in Freddy's garage which was just a few blocks east on Sutton Place. After dropping the two friends off, I was to be taken to my apartment in the Village. I realized that Larry and Freddy must have been good friends for him to use his garage whenever he was in town. Also, while I didn't know a great deal about New York real estate, I had learned that 'the' addresses of the rich and famous in Manhattan were often on

West 57th, lower Fifth Avenue, and Sutton Place. So, if Freddy lived with his momma in a townhouse on Sutton Place, he must have money.

The evening had taught me that homosexuality wasn't limited to starving artists and writers, poor students, would-be actors, and hustlers. It also embraced elegance, talented musicians, and eccentric millionaires, about whom I was anxious to learn more.

A few nights later I received a call from Freddy. "Mr. Cee Jay," he began. "This is Freddy Fuscetti. How are you?"

The purpose of his call was to invite me to a "little dinner gathering" at his townhouse a week from Friday. "I shall be much honored to have the opportunity to know you better than I was able to at my birthday festivities," he said. "Momma shall prepare one of her delicious Italian feasts and my sister Rosa and I shall provide musical entertainment after dinner."

How could anyone not accept an invitation presented in such a way? "Sounds wonderful," I said. "I'll be looking forward to it. Other than your mother and sister, who else are you expecting?" I immediately realized that perhaps that question may have been inappropriate, but I was hoping that this might give me another opportunity to get to know Larry better, if he would be there.

"There will just be six of us at table. Momma, Rosa, you, me, Larry, and Ben. You met Larry and Ben at the club on Friday. Do give Larry a call. He'll be expecting it, so you two can arrange your transportation. Do convince Larry to bring his violin. He and Rosa often accompany me. By the way, Cee Jay, Ben is my brother-in-law. He is Rosa's husband."

I didn't know how quite to respond to that last pronouncement. "I... I understand," I stammered, but I really didn't.

When Freddy and I ended our conversation, I immediately called Larry, who said that I must have just gotten off the phone with Freddy and that he was hoping I had accepted the invitation. Larry said that he would take the Holland Tunnel into the city and that he would be happy to pick me up for the drive to Sutton Place.

At length, I had to ask about Ben. "Freddy said that Ben was his brother-in-law."

"Yes, he is, but if you're asking if he is also a friend of Dorothy, I really am not sure. I've seen him at different clubs and he always seems to be with Jonathan. Jonathan was the one with the camera, the other night. Ben and Freddy seem very comfortable around one another, but beyond that, I don't know the full story." He paused. "The best advice I can give you is to not mention having met him on Freddy's birthday." He paused again. "Cee Jay there are many mysteries surrounding Freddy and his family. I'll fill you in on some of it when I see you on Friday. And I'm sure you'll learn more yourself at Freddy's house."

On the way to Freddy's house on Sutton Place, Larry told me that he and Freddy had lived a few houses from one another in the Ironbound Section of Newark. They had sexually 'fooled around' with one another as pre-adolescents but had remained close friends even though they both moved to different parts of Newark as teenagers. The Fuscetti's moved to Forest Hills and Larry's family moved to 'the Jewish part' of Newark. Larry had bought his own house in Clifton about the same time Mr. Fuscetti bought the Sutton lace property.

"Were you and Freddy ever lovers?" I asked.

"Not in the physical sense," Larry explained. "But, in some ways, I guess you could say we do love one another. We have always shared a love of music. I used to enjoy visiting Freddy at the Forest Hills house. That's where the entire family, including the father, Giuseppe, became enamored with opera. Momma Fuscetti and Rosa both played the piano and sang. Freddy and I would sing together. I guess the Fuscettis were responsible for my interest in the violin and studying music professionally."

"And Giuseppe? Is poppa still alive?"

"No. Sadly he was murdered…. shot. Shortly after they moved to the Sutton Place house. Freddy was only seventeen when he lost his father."

"Horrible! You said he was murdered. Why? By whom?"

"He had been hit by many bullets from many guns; and the murderers took off so quickly, they were never found. Freddy's father was a successful businessman who owned a fleet of trucks that delivered furnace oil to homes and businesses throughout New Jersey and New York. Perhaps Mr. Fuscetti had some enemies, but I don't know about any motive. Neither does Freddy. Fortunately, the townhouse was free and clear of any mortgage at the time of his death, and his brother, who is an attorney, made sure that Momma was well-provided for in Poppa's modest will. The business was sold to the oil corporations."

"Do you suspect, the Mafia may have been involved?"

"Who knows? …. I don't." He paused for a moment of silence between us.

"Remember the club Freddy took us to last week?"

"Sure."

"Well, it's owned by Freddy's Uncle Sal, Giuseppe's brother. Uncle Sal is an attorney for the city. He bought the building for back taxes at auction and renovated it. He set up his own limited liability corporation with himself as president and Freddy's brother-in-law as treasurer. Ben is an accountant. I doubt if Sal has even been in the place, but Freddy and Ben are well-known there, and uncle Sal knows it."

"Wow! As you said on the phone: The family does have a lot of mystery."

We had arrived at the townhouse. "And you probably will discover a few more surprises tonight," Larry said.

The garage door was open, and Larry drove right in. We walked outside to the front and climbed the six steps to a small stoop. Larry rang the doorbell which was loud enough to be heard throughout the house. I was expecting to see the door opened by a tuxedoed butler, but instead. It was Ben who greeted us. In the foyer, he gave Larry a hug and then turned to shake hands with me.

"Good to see you again, Cee Jay," he said softly, removing any fears I had about the relationship issues. "Come in, come in." He led us into the living room, which was all nineteenth century Venetian. Heavy red velvet curtains covered a huge bay window in front of which was a baby grand piano. An ornate marble fireplace occupied most of one wall; on the opposite wall was an over-sized and over-stuffed sofa. A pink, satin chaise lounge sat in the corner by the entrance door. A high back wing chair faced the fireplace. Opposite it on the other side of the fireplace was a large wicker rocking chair. Scattered about the room were small side tables. The two on either side of the sofa had over-sized tiffany-style lamps which I imagine were purchased to match the crystal chandelier which hung from the center of the high ceiling. Surrounding the faded and worn-looking faux- Persian rug the wood floors were pained a shiny black. Two-shades of blue felt flecked wallpaper completed the garish room. From each wall was a quarter wall with two large posts which separated the living room from the dining room which was darkened when we entered the main room.

"Momma Fuscetti and Rosa are still in the kitchen, but will be in to greet you momentarily. Freddy is upstairs doing his final fluff; he'll be sailing down in a minute now that he knows you are here. In the mean- time, may I get you gentlemen a drink?"

Both Larry and I agreed. In order to fathom this room, I definitely needed alcohol. Ben went into the dining room and a moment later wheeled out a cart containing a number of liquors, an ice bucket, a small variety of sodas, and a number of different size glasses.

Larry asked for a seven-and-seven. I requested a gin martini on the rocks with a twist, to which Ben said, "Ah, a man after my own heart. That's my drink also."

All three of us rose when Rosa came in from the kitchen still wearing an apron. She kissed Larry and gave me a warm handshake. "And you must be Mr. Cee Jay. I'm Freddy's sister Rosa Collangelo, I'm always happy to meet my brother's new friends."

"Happy to meet you, Rosa," I said still holding her soft hand. I smiled, "Please just call me Cee Jay. I think Freddy just likes to add the 'Mister' for fun." I got the quick impression that Rosa was a year or two older than her brother, but while Freddy was gushy, she appeared more somber and matronly. "I hope you fellows brought good appetites. Momma and I are going to fatten you up. Larry knows what a great cook momma is. Don't you, Larry?"

We heard Freddy coming down the stairs out in the hall. "Ah, here is my illustrious brother now," Rosa announced.

The Freddy that came into the townhouse parlor immediately seemed different from the man I met at La Bar. First, he seemed fatter. I thought that he may have been wearing a corset last week. His mood was less flamboyant; and instead of fur and a bright green silk scarf, he was soberly attired in a white, long sleeve shirt and black pants. He gave Larry and I a quick embrace.

"Ah, Cee Jay, so good of you to come tonight. I see that you have met Rosa and Ben. Have you met momma yet."

"No, she's still in the kitchen."

To my surprise, Freddy yelled out in a rather macho tone. "Momma! Get in here! Our company's here!" Turning to me, he said, "Momma lives in the kitchen. I have to drag her away some time." Turning to Ben, "Did you make a martini for me?"

"Make your own god damn drinks," was Ben's surprising response.

Where has all the gay pleasantry gone? I asked myself. *Were Freddy and Ben the same two people I met last week?*

Momma Fuscetti came through the dining room. She had a long apron over her black dress. The five of us immediately stood. "Hey, hello, everyone." Spotting me as the new comer, she walked to me bearing a warm smile. "You must be Cee Jay. I'm happy to meet you. Please, sit down, all of you." We did.

"Freddy tells me that he met you at my brother-in-law's bar down town."

I shot a glance to the other men in the room, not knowing how to respond at first. "Ah, yes. I also met Larry down town there." I was hoping that at least Larry would help me out of this awkward situation.

He did. "Yes, momma, Freddy and I were at Uncle Sal's celebrating Freddy's birthday when we ran into Cee Jay. The four of us quickly became friends."

"That's nice. Cee Jay, did Larry tell you that I've known him since he was a little boy? He and my Frederick have been friends for ever. That's why he still calls me momma. Actually, most people call me 'momma.' You can call me 'momma,' too, or 'Marie,' if you prefer. Marie is my real name."

Momma, or Marie, Fuscetti appeared to be in her late sixties or early seventies. She stood about five, five and had snow white hair. I noticed that she wore black nylon stockings and was in navy blue slippers rather than shoes. Surprisingly, while Freddy probably weighed around 250 pounds, she seemed rather moth-eaten at about 110.

Freddy picked up the conversation by asking Larry if had brought his violin. Momma asked Rosa to join her in the kitchen, and as the two passed through the dining room, the chandelier light went on. I noticed that the table was fully set.

Freddy led Larry, Ben, and I to the table. Before sitting down himself, he poured a red wine into the six goblets at each place setting.

The dinner was indeed an Italian feast, starting with an antipasto. The entrée was a delectable veal scaloppini, tortellini, and vegetables. Freddy kept our wine goblets filled through the dessert of spumoni and white cake with expresso. Rosa, who sat next to momma and was closest to the kitchen, did all of the serving.

Momma Fuscetti led the conversation by talking about music and living in Newark. She seemed pleasantly surprised when I told her that I had also at one time lived in the Forest Hill section of the city. She asked if I knew her good friend, an opera singer by the name of Madame Moritza. I had to admit that I did not know the singer and had never met Freddy or Larry while I lived there. Without referring to her husband, it became obvious that momma was much happier living in Newark than she ever was in Sutton Place. She let me know that Freddy, who had taken voice lessons to prepare him as a professional opera singer, had never made it to a stage. He now, however, made a modest income singing at a catholic church in the city on Sundays and occasionally at weddings and funeral masses.

She said that she was still waiting for Rosa and Ben to present her with a grandchild. "You two are not getting any younger, you know," she admonished. "I don't know if Fredrich will ever find the right girl to replace me in his life."

For dessert we had spumoni and a wonderful, moist cake that had a hint of anisette. Eventually, it was Ben who served Sambuca, and we drifted back went into the living room as momma and Rosa cleared the table.

Larry began tuning his violin and talking to Freddy about what he would be singing. Freddy ran through a few scales. Ben and I smiled at one another knowingly. Momma and Rosa reentered the room; momma was no longer wearing her apron but was still in slippers.

The evening's musical entertainment began with Larry and Rosa at the piano playing what I thought was *'Fight of the Bumble Bees.'* Momma then joined Rosa at the piano for a 'four-hand' version of Debussy's *'Claire de lune.'* Larry and Freddy led the clapping when they finished.

This was Freddy's evening to entertain, however. He dedicated his first number to momma, who sat beaming while he sang *'O Sole Mio.'*

As Freddy sang, my eyes roamed above him to the ceiling. I noticed that there was a large rust spot in the corner probably caused by a leak above. A sizable piece of the flecked wallpaper near this spot had loosened and was hanging down. My thoughts drifted from the music to the irony I sudden was aware of. Yes, Giuseppe Fuscetti had provided a townhouse on Sutton Place for his widow, who now probably had no income except for her son's modest salary as a church singer. She and Freddy could live on that I rationalized, if Uncle Sal, her late husband's brother, paid the taxes on this townhouse as a tax break; but only the accountant, Ben Collangelo, would know. It was obvious to me that amid the pretense of supposed wealth and sophistication, there was a real level of poverty. I also wondered if momma had any idea of the kind of 'bar' her brother-in-law owned 'down town' and of which son-in-law Ben was 'treasurer.' Did she have any idea that Ben and her loving son were gay? Perhaps this accounted for Freddy's changed appearance and personality at home versus that at the bars.

Rosa and Larry joined him for his next song. Not being a connoisseur of classical opera, I was thankful that Freddy gave the title and a brief synopsis of '*La donna e Mobile*' from '**Rigoletto**' before doing the solo. I thought that Freddy had an excellent singing voice, and I was really enjoying the experience that he provided me.

Freddy and Rosa ended the evening's entertainment with a song entitled '*Funiculi- Funicula*,' which all of us seemed to enjoy. As I watched Freddy pour his heart and soul into this song, I had to feel sorry for him. Was he not good enough for the Met, so sang to entertain men at his uncle's bar, his friends, members of his small family, and church? How real were his pretentions and affectations or were they his way of peeking out of the closet imposed by his family circumstance? How many men like him would I encounter in La Bar and other watering holes along the way?

Chapter Seven

JOE HOLT

Joe Holt was drop dead gorgeous.

I thought he may have been a hustler because he was standing next to the juke box in the back of the bar where most of them congregated; but I had not seen him here before so I thought that he was either new to the scene or didn't know the unwritten protocols of what one wore, where one stood, and how one stood in La Bar. He did look a bit uneasy. He also looked out of place. No one, whether a regular customer or the hustlers looking for a customer, dressed the way he was dressed. No one came into La Bar in those days wearing cowboy boots and red flannel shirts with red bandanas around his neck. His skin-tight jeans, however, which showed a crotch just too big to be real, were acceptable because it was not unusual in those days for a guy to roll up a sock or two to add to his manly appearance.

Joe Holt was beautiful. His full head of golden, Dutch-boy style hair radiated his tanned, boyish face, which was accented by bright blue eyes. He seemed to exude a boyish innocence even though I guessed him to be about twenty-three. He stood about five seven to five-nine, and was not an ounce over-weight or under- weight. He just stood there with a bottle of beer in his hand which hung down at his side. He seemed unaware of the gazes he must have been receiving, and he seemed not to be paying any attention to anything or anyone around him except the music. Once in a while I saw his head moving up and down as if he were keeping a beat.

I was attracted to this handsome, strange new guy, so when I finished my drink, I decided to head to the restroom but deliberately stopped to get into a conversation with this Adonis. Walking over to him, I decided to be direct.

"Hello, my name is Cee Jay. What's yours?"

"Hi. I'm Joe. Joe Holt."

"You look like a cowboy, Joe Holt."

His smile reminded me of Wally Cleaver. I melted. "Why thaaank ya kindly, sir. I try."

"Ah, you just want to be a cowboy."

"No, sir. I just want to look like a cowboy tonight. It kind a makes me feel sexy."

"Well, I think you are sexy, partner. You're the sexiest god damn cowboy I ever saw here on the plains of ol' N.Y.C.," I said in my best southwestern drawl. I looked down at his sizeable crotch. "You're looking might sexy to me, Joe Holt." He saw where my eyes were and smiled.

"And you look pretty good to me, too, sir."

"Hey, I was just heading out of here. Would you like to go with me to some other watering hole?"

Joe thought about his response for a moment. "Sure. Why not? The night is young." He put his empty beer bottle on the bar. "Let's go."

Outside I took in a deep breath of fresh air and congratulated myself on being brave enough to get him to leave the bar with me. As we slowly walked away, I managed to get a quick glance at his bubble butt. His jeans perfectly contoured to his ass.

"Hey, Joe. Are you wearing anything under those jeans?" I was really feeling brave with this number.

He smiled. "I might let you find out for yourself later, sir."

"emm. I can hardly wait."

"Do you want to go to Marie's Crisis?"

"I may be having a crisis of my own soon. I've never been there, but if it's a bar, sure. Lead the way."

We walked in silence to the bar. I guess we were both trying to figure one another out. Other than the fact that he was cute as hell and called me 'sir,' and was dressed like a cowboy- but wasn't one- I knew nothing about him. And he knew absolutely nothing about me. He must have felt that I was attractive enough for him to go with me so readily. "Hey, Joe. Are you a hustler?" I blurted out.

"Hey, Cee Jay, are you a cop?"

I had to chuckle. "No, I'm a grad student at NYU."

"I thought you were. I'm definitely not a hustler. I work in a bank in midtown. Why did you ask if I were a hustler?"

"Well, for starters, you sure are good looking enough to be one, and La Bar does have its share of call boys. I just wanted to clear the air from the start, that's all."

"Good, because I'd never sell my body; but I'd give it freely to the right man."

At that moment, I realized that my lust for Joe was going to be mixed with some pretty strong feelings.

We arrived at the old, historic piano bar and stepped down the few stairs to enter. Even at 9:30 it was jam packed with men. I volunteered to buy the first round, while Joe would stay at a spot that we found off to the side. It took some time to get served, but when I returned to Joe another, older man was with him. I sensed that they were not having a pleasant conversation.

"Here he is now," Joe said. "I was just telling this man that I was here with my boyfriend and he seems to not want to believe me."

"Seems I can't leave you out of my sight for a minute without someone hitting on you, dear." I smiled as nicely as I could at the guy. "Sorry, mister, he is mine."

The fifty-something man got the message and scurried away without a word.

"Thanks," Joe said.

"For what?"

"For calling me 'dear.'"

"And thank you for telling him I was your boyfriend."

"mmm." Joe took the beer I handed him. I began to sip on my third martini of the Saturday evening.

"So, are we?" I asked letting the alcohol show its effects.

"Are we what?"

"Boyfriends."

Joe seemed to glow. "I don't know…. Maybe later. …Too soon to tell, though"

"You're right. So, Joe Holt, tell your 'maybe later' boyfriend more about yourself."

"You know I work in midtown, but I have an apartment in Weehawken, New Jersey."

"I'm from New Jersey also, but now that I'm at NYU, I have an apartment here in the Village. Do you live alone in Weehawken or do you live with family?"

"Ah, still trying to 'clear the air'?" he said. "I live alone, so yeah, I am available. I have a small one bedroom. The rent is outrageous, but it's a great building and I have a great view of Manhattan. The rent for a similar apartment in Manhattan would be much more than I could afford. The commute to the bank I am working in isn't bad. I actually prefer living in New Jersey, but I'm close enough when I went to."

"What do you do at the bank?"

"I handle the international currency exchange department."

I smiled. "Well, there goes the fantasy of having a cowboy as a boyfriend."

"I do like playing dress-up. I could be anything you want me to, Cee Jay." His smile was absolutely adorable. "You should see my collection of gowns."

We finished our drinks at the same time. "Would you like a refill," I asked.

"No, not right now, thanks. I'm afraid that if I had another beer right now, you wouldn't like me."

"Good, because I've reached my limit also." I paused. "Would you like to see my messy fourth floor walk-up?"

"Sure."

Wow! This guy doesn't need much encouragement, I thought. *Tonight's my lucky night.*

The pace of our walk back to my apartment was much faster than our walk to Marie's Crisis, but I was able to discover that Joe had graduated from Jersey City State College two years ago, and he learned that I was majoring in English literature and educational administration.

By the time we climbed to the fourth floor of my building and I got the door open, we were both panting. I don't know if the panting was caused by the fast walk and climb of stairs or our mutual lust, but once inside the closed doors, we immediately began devouring one another.

Joe holt was a great kisser. I directed him into the bedroom. "Sir, you will be gentle with me, won't you? I do depend on the kindness of strangers."

"Okay Blanche Dubois." I gently pushed him down on the bed. "Why do you call me 'sir'?"

"Because I like a man to take charge. I want to please you, sir. I can tell you like it. Don't you, sir? Being dominant?"

Joe Holt did hit a cord with me. I realized that, yes, I did like to take charge in a sexual situation. I never liked a partner to tell me what to do, how to do it, and how to position myself. I liked to explore, and if the guy didn't like what I was doing, he didn't have to tell me. I knew instinctively to stop. Bossy sex partners were definitely a turn-off for me. Joe was the perfect submissive, but I certainly wasn't a dominant master either. 'S' and 'M' just wasn't my scene, but I did like a sex partner to follow, not lead.

I led by removing his boots. Then undoing his big belt buckle and reaching inside his pants with my fingers...

"Earlier you asked if I were wearing underwear. Do you have the answer?"

I stood at the side of the bed and continued to undo his fly. "Yep, white jockey shorts are a bit of a fetish with me."

"Sorry, partner. They're Haines." He grabbed my belt and pulled me closer.

I pulled off my shoes and got on the bed. I put my arms around him and held him like a precious child, which he was. We kissed, we petted, we slowly and erotically removed one another's clothes. I could not remember ever having had sex so slowly as I did with Joe Holt that night or with anyone ever since. I loved making love to Joe and he reciprocated 100%. If I would play with his nipples, a minute later he was sucking on mine. When I eventually went down to taste his big manhood, he did the same to me a few minutes later.

Coming with Joe was like a release into heaven. Yes, I could hear the angels singing, and see the stars. There were no fireworks, just shear bliss and utter content. We lay side by side holding hands in naked silence.

Eventually, Joe got up. "Gotta hit your little boy's latrine, partner," he said. He didn't have to be told where it was. The only light was from the living room floor lamp which I had turned on when we first entered the apartment, but Joe found the bathroom. A few minutes later, he returned with a wash cloth and towel. He gently washed the cum on my penis, hands, and belly and gently padded me dry with the towel. He then tossed both on the chair and lay down beside me.

He took the initiative this time of taking me in his arms and deep throating me. Again, our sex play was slow, sensual, and wonderful. We came at the same time again.

"Wow! Cowboy, you sure are one wild stallion."

"I'm glad I please you, sir."

I stood up and took his hand. "Come on let's take a shower together."

"Sounds good to me, sir."

In the shower he waited while I adjusted the faucets for the best temperature before pulling him into the claw tub with me. We kissed passionately. Seeing the water run down his face, was a total turn on and grabbed his beautiful, angelic face with both hands and began kissing him again. We washed one another's cocks and backs. I enjoyed running my hands all over his cute, little butt and actually running the bar of soap up and down and inside his crack. I began playing with his pink pucker and was delighted to see that he responded so positively to my explorations. He moaned. "Yes, sir. I do like it, sir." I was stiff once again, so I positioned him in a way that I could cock tease his ass hole without actually penetrating. I reached around to hold his enlarged piece. When he pressed his body to mine, I felt as if we were merging into one. He turned his head slightly so that we could kiss. We stayed locked in this embrace until the water was too cold to continue.

As we dried one another with the same towel, Joe broke the silence. "I guess I better be getting back to Weehawken. The Path really slows down late at night."

I was suddenly startled by the realization that Joe would leave me. Back in the bedroom, I checked my watch. "My god. It's nearly two o'clock. I had no idea we were at it so long." I couldn't let Joe leave. "Why don't you stay here for the night?"

"Okay," was all he said. We both got back into the bed and again began making passionate love. This time, however,

I indicated that I wanted to fuck this cowboy. His moaning "mmms" told me it was okay with him too. "We'll need some KY. Have some?" Joe asked.

I leaned over to get my tube in the night stand drawer. Joe got up and took something out of a pocket in his jeans which had been left on the floor. "Hope you don't mind my using poppers."

I looked at the little vile he showed me. "What's this?"

"It's an inhaler. A lot of guys use poppers at discos. It's really amyl nitrite and is used to speeds up your heart. You never saw or used it before? I think it stinks like hell, but it does help me to loosen my ass up."

"Is it a drug?"

"I don't know, but you can buy it in just about any store in the Village. I'm surprised that you never heard of poppers before. Some people simply call it Rush. The trouble is that the high- or rush- is very short. Here, you want to try it?"

"No thanks. I'll pass." The mere thought of using an inhaler- drug or no drug- at the time was a turn-off for me. It just seemed a bit unnatural. I reacted by getting soft and inactive. I stayed still thinking about this for some time. After a while, however, Joe took the initiative of arousing me and made sure it was hard enough. He did not use the inhaler even though he had some difficulty accepting me. Once I was fully in, we both came easily for the third orgasm of the night.

We both quickly fell asleep locked in an embrace.

The telephone ringing woke us both up. A quick glance at the clock/radio indicated that it was 9:30, so I rolled out of bed and went into the living room to answer the call. It was Paul inviting me to their apartment for mimosas and quiche with eggs.

"Ah, I'd like to Paul, but I have company."

"Company? Like a trick, company?"

"Yes."

"And he stayed over- night? I want to hear all about him."

"Later, okay. Actually, we both were asleep. You woke me up. I don't know about him."

"Well, good god, man, It's almost 10:00. Get him out of your bed and bring him down here for breakfast. I was going to call Diane, to join us; but your new number may fill the extra place nicely. Go ask him."

I looked back into the bedroom and saw that Joe was very much awake and leaning on his elbow looking at me quizzically. "It's a friend who lives one floor below. He wants to know if we'll join him and his lover for breakfast in their apartment."

"Sure, but we'll need at least a half-hour to get our acts together. I'd like to meet your friends."

"Paul, you still there?"

"Of course. I heard every word of your little conversation. George and I will see you at 10:15. By the way, what is your new boyfriend's name?"

"Joe."

"I hope Joe isn't a priest or rabbi or something like that last number you had."

"No. He works in a bank. See you in forty-five minutes. Thanks for the invite."

I did a quick shave with my electric; Joe said his natural blonde peach fuzz was okay as is. We gargled with mouthwash and took a quick shower. I got into fresh underwear, a polo and khakis while Joe had to shake out his jeans and shirt in an attempt to get the bar smoke odor out.

"Next time I come here, I'll bring a change of clothes."

My jaw may have dropped. "Does that mean that my cowboy is now a boyfriend?"

"That's still a big maybe; but I'm willing to work on it, if you are."

I took him in my arms and we kissed warmly despite the lingering taste of Listerine.

My third- floor neighbors were their usual charming selves. Paul came into the living room wearing a long apron and George had a freshly-made pitcher of mimosas at the ready.

"So, I want to know all about how you two met," Paul gushed. "Knowing Cee Jay, I bet it was at La Bar."

"Yep, that's about it. Cee Jay came up to me, we talked a little and then went to Marie's Crisis for a drink and then he invited me to his place."

"And?" Paul indicated with his hand that he wanted to know more.

"And then Cee Jay asked me to stay over. It was too late for me to go back to Weehawken where I live." There was a hesitant minute of silence in the room.

George realized that was all either Joe or I were going to tell at the time. "More wake-up juice?" he asked going for the pitcher and filling our flutes.

"Breakfast will be on the table shortly," Paul said. As he took his glass into the kitchen.

"So, you're from New Jersey, Joe. I was born and raised in Bayonne," George said.

"No kidding? I lived there for a while myself before we moved to Jersey City. My father owned a bar on Kennedy Boulevard. It was called 'Holt's. That's my last name."

"Sure. I know Holt's. I never was in it, but I know of it. I passed it often on the bus. I thought it was in Jersey City, though."

"Very near the border, but in Bayonne." Joe turned to me. "Bayonne has more bars than churches, and it has a lot of churches."

"Big Roman Catholic Polish population. Is it still that way?" George asked.

Joe chuckled. "That describes me, but I haven't been in Bayonne since pop sold the bar."

Paul called from the kitchen that breakfast was ready and we went into the kitchen. On the way in, Joe noticed the baseball pennants on the wall over the bed. Before sitting down at the table, he made notice also of the curtain separating the table from the rest of the kitchen.

During breakfast, I began to notice that Joe seemed to become more aloof or withdrawn. His demeanor reminded me of the way he stood at the bar before I introduced myself to him. I also noticed that he was downing the mimosas at a much quicker rate than the three of us. Paul had been refilling his flute without comment, but when Joe actually took the pitcher and emptied its contents into his own glass, I noticed that Paul shot me a raised eyebrow. I kind of twisted my mouth in nonverbal questioning to indicate that I shared Paul's concern.

I was glad that George did not volunteer to make another pitcher of mimosas. I felt that the drinks were strong enough; he must have put an entire bottle of champagne into that one pitcher. Joe did not have any coffee, but instead slowly finished his mimosa. He twisted the flute around a few times in the air the way a wine taster might swirl his glass. I got the impression that he was hinting that he wanted another. I also noticed that he became fidgety and kept readjusting himself in his chair. He seemed uncomfortable.

"I better start getting back to New Jersey," Joe said as soon as he saw that we were finished with our coffees.

There was something wrong, but I had no idea what it was. I could sense that Paul realized the awkwardness in the room too. All four of us got up from the table simultaneously. At the door, George and Paul shook hands with Joe. He thanked them for the breakfast. I did the same. When the door was closed, I just shook my head and thought *'What the hell just happened in there? Joe was practically running out of the apartment. Why?'*

"Would you like to come upstairs for a while?"

"No need. I have everything. I would like you to walk with me to the PATH station on Christopher Street, though."

"Okay. I could use the exercise and fresh air." I also felt that I wanted to get some understanding of what was bothering Joe. The Village sidewalks were quiet on Sunday mornings and the air was clear and cool. We passed a restaurant that had tables outside. I was aware that most of those having brunch were straight, tourists and couples who lived in the area. The gay denizens were probably still in bed or nursing hangovers. All the bar/restaurants were busy, however. We passed a popular, old such establishment.

Joe tugged at my jaket. "Let's go in here and have a bloody mary. They make 'em good in here."

"What? It's only a little after one and we had mimosas for brunch."

"Yeah, but now I'm in the mood for a bloody mary." He nearly shoved me into the place.

"Come on. I'll treat."

He's in the 'mood' for a bloody mary this early in the afternoon. I have no idea what his 'mood' really is, I thought.

The restaurant was quaint; it had a pot belly stove in a back corner and dark wood wainscoting. It had a tin ceiling. A round table for four was at a window on either side of the door. The other tables in the room were for two people. All the tables were occupied. A lone man was reading the *New York Times* on one of the four stools at the small bar in the back. He was either waiting to be joined by a friend or just waiting to be seated by himself. Joe led the way to the bar.

A waiter quickly appeared. "Will you gentlemen be waiting for a table?"

"No," Joe said. "We'll just have two bloody marys." On the bar was a container for pencils and the restaurant/bar's business cards. On the back of the cards, conveniently printed was 'Name' and 'Telephone' for any trick you may meet there. Joe wrote his name and telephone number for me on one of the cards; he gave me another one and asked me to write my telephone number. "Numbers for numbers exchange," he said as I gave him the card.

I slowly drank the bloody mary, while Joe polished off two drinks in the same time.

"Joe, last night at Marie's you said that I might not like you if you had another drink. What did you mean by that?"

"Simple. You might think I was an alcoholic." He seemed belligerent. "But I'm not. I can handle my booze." He spun around on the stool to look over the people in the restaurant. He said nothing more, but eventually put his empty glass on the bar. "I better take a piss before we leave," he said. As he was walking to the one restroom in the restaurant, I noticed that he was wobbling and obviously not 'handling his booze' as well as he thought.

We walked in silence the short distance to the PATH station on Christopher but on the opposite side of the street. I went down the stairs to the platform with him to make sure he would not fall more than to bid a fond farewell. At the turnstiles I did embrace him, however. "I'll call you," he said as we heard the train approaching.

As soon as I got back to my apartment I called George and Paul. I again wanted to thank them for the nice breakfast, but more importantly to talk about Joe's strange behavior after meeting them.

Paul answered the phone. "Did you get your cutie pie on the train okay?"

"Yeah, I went to the station with him, but…."

"Yes, but?"

"Paul, Joe seemed very different in your apartment from the way he was last night. I was wondering if you noticed anything unusual about him."

"Since you bring it up, George and I were curious about him. He is a really good- looking guy, but…"

It was my turn to finish. "But what?" Paul's response was not quick in coming. "Paul, are you still there?"

"Yes, I'm here. Cee Jay, you might not like to hear this, but both Dip shit and I think that he may be a drug addict."

"Drug addict! Why do you say that?"

"He may have needed a fix. We both thought he got a bit agitated and fidgety, and he did practically run out of our apartment. And rather than going back to your place for a little snuggling or whatever, he just wanted out. Those are usually signs of a druggie. Did he give you any indication?"

"No, not really; but, Paul, do you know anything about poppers? He had an inhaler and asked me if I wanted a snort."

Paul chuckled. "Cee Jay, you mean to tell me that you have never used Rush?"

"No, I never even heard about it until last night. I kind of indicated to Joe that I didn't like the idea, so he put the inhaler away without using it. Do you think he may be addicted to poppers?"

"I never heard of any one being addicted to amyl. Many guys use it occasionally. A few times I've used it with Dipshit, but he can't stand the smell. He claims it gives him a headache. It's used mostly at discos or when you are about to come."

"Well, honestly, last night we both came three times and it was great, and neither of inhaled that shit."

"Okay. Do you have any thoughts about his behavior?"

"Paul, the guy drank a lot of mimosas this morning."

"Yeah, we all noticed that."

"And before we got to the Christopher PATH station, he insisted on going into a bar and having two bloody marys."

"Wow! Your new boyfriend may not be a druggie, but an alcoholic. Be careful, Cee Jay. Either way, he could be difficult." He paused. "But he sure is cute."

After speaking with Paul, I was quite despondent. It was difficult for me to accept the fact that Joe, who was so attractive, who seemingly liked me as well, who seemed so innocent, and a sweet guy, and great in bed on Saturday, could possibly be a drug addict or alcoholic.

It wasn't until Monday morning that I came to the reality of the fact that I was not living in Greenwich Village to straighten out my sexual preferences or to find a life partner. I was there to attend New York University and earn a doctor of education degree. I had to stop thinking of guys, particularly Joe Holt. Going to classes was helpful in the process. By Monday evening I was completely concentrating on my studies.

I was engaged in reading when my phone rang late Tuesday evening. It was Joe. He sounded like the Joe I knew and made love to on Saturday. He apologized for his behavior on Sunday morning. He reminded me of what he had said in Marie's Crisis about not liking him if he had too much to drink. He was so direct and sincere that I told him that I did understand and hoped that he would not over-do drinking in the future.

He told me that the reason he drank so much at Paul and George's place was that he felt awkward and ill-at-ease with them and thought that by drinking he could take the edge off his nervousness among new people, particularly my friends that were new to him. He then asked if I would go to his apartment on Saturday. He said that I should come early and he would make dinner for us to eat in his place.

"That sounds great, Joe, but I have a class I must attend on Saturday and a study group in the late afternoon, so Saturday is not possible," I said. "Could we do it on Sunday afternoon instead, but I'd have to get back to the Village no later than ten o'clock."

"Sunday seems much too far away, but if it has to be Sunday, I'll have to settle. I miss you so much, Cee Jay. I've been going crazy thinking about you the last two days. When can you get here on Sunday?"

"Just give me directions and your apartment number. I'll be there about two o'clock on Sunday, if that's okay."

He tried to make it earlier, but after the directions, etc. it was agreed that I would be at his place at two o'clock.

On Saturday I started work on a paper that was due on Monday morning. The report required more research than I originally expected, so I burned the midnight oil trying to get it finished; but at eleven o'clock I was still not finished and completely exhausted. I was determined, however, to finish it as early as possible so that I could visit with Joe without worrying about the damn homework paper.

I woke up early and got started on my assignment as quickly as possible; but still only managed to finish it by noon. I shaved, showered and got dress and left my apartment by one. I reasoned that it shouldn't take me more than an hour to get on the other side of the Hudson River. Joe suggested that rather than taking the PATH into Jersey City, it might be better to go to the Port Authority Bus Terminal and take a bus directly to his apartment building on Kennedy Boulevard in Weehawken. What we did not count on, however, was that on Sundays that particular bus didn't run as frequently. I had to wait until 2:10 for the next bus and was told at the ticket counter that it would not get to Joe's stop until 2:55 because it made a stop in Jersey City. I was concerned that I would be about an hour late. I didn't want Joe to think that I was standing him up, but I had no control over the bus schedule. I reasoned that, if he were worried, he might try calling me at home and realize that I was out- trying to get to his place.

Finally, the bus driver called out the stop. Joe said that he lived in a round building and I would be left off in front of it. The building was modern and completely round; looking up at this high rise, I figured it must have had at least twenty stories. Joe said his apartment number was 1504, so I guessed he must have lived on the fifteenth floor. A concierge behind a marble counter greeted me with the usual 'May I help you, sir.' I told him I was here to visit 1504. He picked up a phone while asking for my name.

"Mr. Holt? Mr. Cee Jay Seton is here to see you. Yes, sir," he paused momentarily. "I will tell him that. Should I send him up?"

Putting down the phone, he looked a bit puzzled. "He told he to inform you that you are an hour late, but said that you should go on up any way."

Joe greeted me warmly as soon as I rang the bell. "So, you finally got here. What kept you so long? You know you are an hour late."

"Yes, I know. Your doorman also had to remind me."

"You're damn straight!" He practically shouted at me and took me off guard.

"I'm sorry, Joe. I thought it would only take an hour to get here, but apparently they run fewer buses from the Port Authority to Weehawken on Sundays."

I was beginning to feel uncomfortable and began thinking I had made a mistake in making the trip to see him. I wondered if he was going to remain the same surly character he was at Paul and George's apartment last Sunday. "So, aren't you glad I made it?"

"Sure, but you damn well better be here when you say you will in the future. You were probably cruising the tea room in the terminal."

He had led me down a small hall into his living room. His last remark was ignored as I saw the fantastic view he had of the entire Manhattan skyline. "Wow! You have a great view here." I walked directly over to the windows. The panorama stretched from the Verrazano Bridge all the way passed the George Washington Bridge. Joe came behind me and wrapped his arms around me.

"I watched them building this complex and knew that I wanted to live here. That is a million- dollar view. Wait until later when the lights of the city go on. I almost like it better at night."

"I bet. You can watch all the cruise ships coming and going. Really fantastic!"

"Come on, I'll show you around. The living room was shaped as an 'L' with the dining area at the other end. His dining room was furnished with a white, round table with four white leather chairs. The wall was covered with a white shag carpet with an abstract pattern of red, yellow, orange, and brown. It was very modern and I told him that I liked it. He had set the table with dishes, glasses, napkins, and a large candle.

"I guess we are having dinner in this afternoon," I said.

"Yep. I want you to learn what a great cook your new boyfriend is." He smiled at me. He was so cute, when he wanted to, I almost felt like kissing him.

"Hey, look down. You see those trees and bushes down there?"

"Yes."

"That's Weehawken's answer to Central Park. The cruising in the woods there has more action, and the cops never chase guys out of the bushes. There are some park benches on the patio around the building and you can watch who is taking a little stroll into the woods and follow."

"And does cowboy Joe also go on scouting trips?" I said jokingly.

He looked at me with another big smile. "Is the pope catholic?" he responded.

The kitchen included a dish washer and a small desk area that could be used as a breakfast table. I took note of the pots, pans, etc. that were on the stove and bowls that were waiting to be used on the counter space. The other end of the galley kitchen had a door that opened to the entry hall. A door on the left was for a generous size closet and next to it was a large bathroom. The bedroom was across the hall. It, too, had windows that extended from one wall to the other and afforded the same magnificent views as the living room. Other than a slight curve at the windows, the apartment belied the fact that the building was round.

Joe's place was small and sparsely furnished, but what furniture Joe had was appropriate for the space. It was modern and gave his apartment a comfortable feel. Back in the living room I sat down on a small sofa that backed against the windows and faced a long, narrow table which Joe used as an entertainment center that had a television, radio, and a phonograph turn table. Speakers were separated to the far ends of the wall. Under the table were many 33 and 1/3rd albums. Every gay guy's apartment I had been in had the obligatory liquor cart, and Joe's was no exception.

"I know you like gin martinis, so look what I got just for you." He picked up a bottle on the cart and brought it over to show mw. "Tanqueray is the best gin. I prefer Stolli for my vodka martinis. On the rocks or straight?" he asked.

"Oh, definitely with ice. With a lemon twist, if you have."

"Sure, a good bartender has twists. I myself like olives." I noticed that he took great care in making our drinks. He rubbed the rim of my glass with the lemon and made sure it was only a drop of dry vermouth. I wondered, however, how many drinks he may have had while waiting for me.

"I thought you were a bloody mary man."

"I do like 'bloodies,' but a vodka martini is better before dinner. Bloody marys remind me of Fire Island and P' town. I love to drink them and look out at the ocean."

"Paul and George told me about Fire Island. We plan on going out there this summer. But where is P' town? I never heard of it." He handed me my drink.

"P' town is Provincetown, Massachusetts. All the New York faggots go to Jones Beach or Fire Island on weekends and to the Cape for a week's vacation. You've never been to Cape Cod?"

"I've only discovered the gay scene a few months ago." I had to smile. "I'm practically a virgin, Joe."

"Well, you must be a fast learner because you were expert at it last Saturday. Maybe you and I could get up to P' town this summer. You would love it. It's kind of a rustic and quaint old fishing village. Deserted in the winter, but crawling with hot faggots in the summer. The beach is wild."

I thought for a moment. "I read somewhere that the playwright Eugene O'Neil had a theater in Provincetown."

"Yeah, there is a theater there. It's right on the pier. Theater on one side and a gay disco on the opposite side."

"It sounds very nice. I'll keep it in mind for a trip next summer."

We sat in silence for some time, before Joe asked how I liked the drink he made for me.

"It's perfect. Much better than at La Bar."

"That's because they use cheap, well gin. Tanqueray makes the difference."

"You really know how to make drinks, Joe. Did you learn bartending from your father?"

"Nah, my pop's bar was strictly shots and beer. Before he sold the dump, I had ideas of turning it around, hoping to make it a gay bar maybe. I went to a mixology school in Jersey City to make the fancy drinks; but then the old man wanted to sell his place, and I couldn't afford to buy him out. Just as well, I guess. Instead, I was able to finish college."

Joe walked to me and stood. He bent down and kissed me. The taste of liquor was on his lips and mouth. "I hope you're hungry, because we're going to have a fine Sunday dinner. Why don't you pick out some music while I finish cooking?" He abruptly turned to head into the kitchen, but stopped at his liquor cart to replenish his drink.

I knelt at the table under which Joe's albums were stored. Joe's tastes in music were apparent: folk, country and western, and disco. My own preference of show and classical were completely absent. In his collection among other artists of the day, I found Pete Seeger, Kris Kristofferson, Woody Guthrie, Lucy and Carly Simon, Tom Chapin, Billy Joel, and Judy Collins. I called to Joe in the kitchen. "In the mood for a bit of Judy Collins?"

Joe came back into the living room. "Sure. I'll show you how to put it on. mmm. "Both Sides Now.' Interesting choice."

"Yes, Diane and I were listening to her sing just last week at the Village Gate."

"Who's Diane?"

She lives in my building. George and Paul introduced her to me and we get together occasionally. Paul calls her our 'resident fag hag.'"

"I can't stand fag hags, and I can't stand your fucking pal Paul either."

I was shocked to hear him speak so negatively of two people that I liked. "What don't you like about Paul?"

"He's just too damn girlish for me. I can't stand a piss elegant fag who thinks he's better than me. Aren't him and that Georgie boy of his the cutest couple living in their cheap, run-down apartment and putten on airs."

"Joe, what are you talking about: 'putting on airs'? I live in that same cheap, run-down building. They are friends of mine."

"That god damn curtain across their kitchen nearly made me puck. Only fags would try to hide their old kitchen by trying to create some kind of a café. And only a frat fairy would have all those college pennants over his bed."

At the moment I thought it best to drop the conversation entirely and put on the record, so I got up and went to the phonograph player. I was hurt, but didn't want to start a scene that would turn an already questionable afternoon into a worse one. In silence Joe put the recording on, turned up the volume, and went back to the kitchen. I really had the feeling that he was itching for a fight, but had no idea why. One minute he seemed nice; and the next, he seemed angry and mad.

The dinner was excellent. Joe had made each of us another martini. We touched glasses in a sort of toast. We started with a Caesar salad with baby shrimp. After which, Joe got up to make himself another drink. He offered me one, but I had hardly touched mine, so I passed. The entrée consisted of London broil smothered in au juice, big baked potatoes with sour cream, and fresh carrots.

I asked Joe how he learned to cook. He told me that his mother had died when he was still in high school, so his sister who was a few years older did most of the cooking for him and his father. What culinary skills he had came mostly from his sister. Dad was seldom home because his days and nights were spent running the bar.

As Joe spoke, I began to notice that he was slurring his words. There were several dull moments in the conversation. He seemed distracted, so I asked about his sister. "Did your sister Rose get married?"

"Yeah, she married some god-damn pollack she met at my old man's bar."

"Do they still live in Bayonne?"

"Nah. They rent in Jersey City. Have two beautiful kids though… a boy and a girl."

"Ah, is Uncle Joe proud of his nephew and niece?"

"Kind a. Say, why are you so god-damn inner-ested in my fucking family? You more inner-ested in em than me?"

"No, Joe, but if I'm to get to know you, I guess I'm just curious about your family."

He pushed back on his chair. "Well, I don't give a shit about your family and you shouldn't about mine!" he shouted as he staggered over to his liquor cart for another drink. This time he didn't ask if I wanted a refill.

Coming back to the table he nearly fell into his chair. "You want some dessert?" he said at last.

"Sure. After such a big meal, I guess an extra couple of hundred calories would do no harm." I smiled, hoping for a lighter atmosphere. "What are we having?"

At first Joe didn't say anything, then he turned toward the refrigerator and waved his hand in that direction. "Help yourself. It's on a shelf in the frig."

I wondered at this point if Joe could stand up, so I went to the refrigerator myself and easily found two dishes containing angel food cakes covered with sliced peaches. Returning to the table, I saw that Joe's chin was pressing into his chest and his hand was gripping the glass. I thought that he may have fallen asleep or passed out from too much liquor. I put his dessert in front of him. "Joe!" I practically shouted as I rubbed his shoulders. He seemed startled and shook his body.

"Get your fucking hands off me! Are you trying to molest me?"

I sat down. "Joe, would you like me to make some coffee for us?"

"No, for me," he stammered. "You make fo you self, if you want." His chin dropped into his chest again.

I had one or two bites of the cake and peaches, but just was no longer interested in eating. Joe did not touch the dessert. My concern was about getting Joe away from falling over the table or worse falling on the floor.

"Come on, Joe. Let's get you into a chair in the living room." Going behind him, I put my hands under his arms and used my full strength to get him standing. He almost fell into me as he put his arms around me. I kicked the chair aside and very carefully managed to get him into the closest chair, a recliner in the living room. I guided his fall into it and sat on the sofa. Neither of us spoke for some time.

I knew now that Joe Holt was an alcoholic. I knew that some guys, myself included, drank to be more social, to have a good time, or to loosen up a bit. Joe was the first person I ever met who drank to excess and, in doing so, had major mood swings. One minute he could be sweet and charming and, after a few drinks become a 'Jekyll and Hyde' nasty sort of changed personality. I liked the soft spoken, cute and charming, Joe; but I did not have the ability to handle the intoxicated, pugnacious Joe I now realized he was.

Joe stirred out of the chair and staggered out of the room. "Gotta piss," he mumbled as he bumped into the wall leading into the bathroom in the hall. He did not close the bathroom door.

After he finished urinating, I heard nothing more. I sat, dazed and confused, wondering what I should do. After a few minutes I got up and went to see if he was okay. The bathroom light was still on and the door was open. I looked into Joe's bedroom and found him fully clothed but passed out in a fetal position on the bed. I saw that he had not zippered his fly.

"Joe," I called softly. "Joe, are you okay?" Going close to him, I could tell that he was still breathing heavily, but obviously sound asleep.

I went back into the living room and near the telephone, I found a directory and a pen. I tore a page out of the spiral directory and wrote a short note. "Joe," I wrote, "Thanks for the very good dinner. I'm glad I got to see your great apartment. I have to get back to the City (early classes tomorrow). Give me a call sometime. Stay well. Cee Jay."

I left the note attached to the mirror in the bathroom, flushed the toilet, and turned the light out. As quietly as possible, I opened the door to the apartment and closed it- and Joe Holt- out of my life.

Chapter Eight

THE CRACK OF THE BAT

Everything and everyone in the park was silent. The jeering and yelling of good wishes stopped. There was a stillness in the April air as George began his wind up.

Then there was the crack of the bat!

For a split second I thought George turned slightly to glimpse to his right to see if his shortstop was ready for the line drive.

In "The Waste Land" T.S. Eliot wrote: "April is the cruelest month." Ever since that day in Bloomfield years ago, when April comes, I can hear the crack of that bat and envision once again the blood, the crying, and confusion of that particular early April day.

Bob Fielding, the manager of the La Bar team, was contacted by the team from Asbury Park to play an early spring "work-out" game. Bob checked with the guys from the bar, and within a week the game was planned for the following Saturday in the park in Bloomfield, New Jersey. Paul asked Diane and me if we would take the two of them and some equipment to Jersey; we readily agreed Early that Saturday Diane and I went to the parking lot where she kept her '55 Chevy. We drove the few blocks to wait in front of our apartment building for the guys.

Diane explained to me that before she bought the car, a previous owner painted it a tangerine color, a color she approved of in the 1960's; but the car was frequently in need of repair, so she nicknamed it "the tangerine lemon." As a result, we never referred to Diane's car as 'Diane's car.' It was always 'Diane's tangerine lemon.'

"You know, I don't feel good about this," Diane said.

Her statement was so sudden and unrelated to what we had been talking about, I was stunned for a moment. "What do you mean, Diane? It's a beautiful morning. Perfect for baseball. Maybe it's a bit too warm for this time of year."

"Perhaps that's it. It's just too damn warm for this time of year. It's strange." She paused. "Anyway, I feel just a bit creepy."

George and Paul appeared in their freshly washed blue and white striped uniforms. The guys looked like real professionals- Yankees or Dodgers- rather than queer men from a Village bar who were out to play for the mere sport of the game rather than fame and fortune. A quick thought entered my mind: I wondered how many closet gays were in professional baseball. Diane and I got out of the car to open the trunk and help put in the ice chest filled with ice and bottles of Gatorade as well as their bats and a few balls. Like respectful young boys might, Paul and George removed their caps that had "La Bar" embroidered on the visors and placed them over the balls to keep them from rolling. I also thought that perhaps they also didn't want to be too obvious to the collectors at the toll booth at the Holland Tunnel.

"How's that arm of yours?" Diane asked as she drove off.

"Great!" George replied. "I'm ready to pitch the perfect game today. Too bad that Steinbrenner won't get to see my magnificence, though. Only that hunky Bloomfield cop and a few kids on their bikes will stop and ask for my autograph."

"Yeah, you wish," Paul chided. "I think you wish you could give more than your autograph to that cop."

"Well, if you can keep your mind off hot policemen and do your job as shortstop, we may kick some Asbury Park ass this afternoon.' He paused before adding, "and you know that I only have eyes for you, dear."

Paul leaned over and ran his hand through his lover's crew cut. "Sure. I know you do, Dip shit." I turned around to see the two baseball players smiling with an expression not unlike a cat who just swallowed a canary. At that moment I knew that these two truly loved one another, and at the same moment, I felt envious of them for that love.

Now it was Diane's turn to enter into the banter. "I do wonder if he'll be out in his patrol car again this season saving innocent boys from you guys. If he's there this summer, I'm going to ask him for a date."

"What! You want to break the fantasy and actually talk to the nice officer? George, tell her that he's mine."

The conversation continued in a similar fashion through the tunnel, but once in New Jersey the two players began to talk about their opponents and what they could expect if the same players for the Asbury Park team were still on it. They were mentioning names, statistics, and strengths and weaknesses of their opponents. All the gay bantering was over; George in particular seemed intent on the upcoming game and how the men from La Bar were going to defeat the crew from the Jersey shore.

Diane, meanwhile, was concentrating on the confusing signs of the myriad of highways stemming from the tunnel into Jersey City and beyond. I could tell that the Saturday traffic was making her nervous. She seemed to be driving like someone with a precious cargo. She was: Her two best friends in the world were in the back. I was grateful to be part of that company. Diane's tension seemed to ease when we got on the Garden State Parkway, a toll road. "I wonder what those fuckers down in Trenton do with all the money they collect on this road," she said. "You'd think they would have paid for the damn road by now. By the way gentlemen, I hope your sponsors pay me for gas and tolls."

The last toll was at the Bloomfield exit. We made a left onto Bloomfield Avenue and went back under the Parkway. All our eyes immediately caught sight of the black and white police car parked on the grass at the edge of the park and the avenue.

"Is that your Officer Krupke in that police car? I asked.

"Oh, I'm sure it was," Paul bellowed. "Didn't you see him blow me a kiss as we went through the intersection?"

"Whoever was in that car seems to be looking out for speeders and light jumpers. The hunky one usually parks up by the restrooms, not at the corner," Diane said. "Didn't Bob Fielding notify the city that we were playing here today?"

"He or the manager from Asbury Park should have," George replied. "If not, we may be paying a fine…. and Diane can't pay a fine on top of everything else."

"Yeah, right!" Diane said as she made a left at the I-Hop on the next corner. She turned onto the single-lane paved road that circled around the restroom building and the entire park which enclosed a large apartment complex and ran aside the embankment for the Garden State Parkway before opening up again on the other side of the apartment buildings.

She parked the tangerine lemon behind the restrooms. Several cars, including a van that was painted in blue and white to represent ocean waves with a large sign that read "Asbury Park's Finest Men," were parked around the building. The baseball field that was used for league games was just to the left and below the stone and brick restroom building. Home plate was a few feet in front of a batter's cage. The pitcher's mound and the three bases were clearly set, but the rest of the field was all grass. The managers, coaches and the umpires usually determined what would be considered foul lines and a home run.

After the usual handshakes and a few hugs, the game began.

The Asbury Park team was up first. I remember how well George was pitching considering that he had not thrown in several months. He struck out the first two batters he faced, but the third batter hit a ground ball which Paul picked up and threw to first base, arriving seconds after the batter who slid in successfully for a single. The next man up swung twice but connected on George's third pitch for a high pop into right field. It was caught and the side was retired. The La Bar guys struck out and popped out to make the score nothing-nothing at the end of the first inning.

The two teams seemed about evenly matched, and the score remained zero for both sides through four complete innings. The only bit of excitement in the game to that point came during the third inning when Paul attempted to steal second base but was called out.

Diane and I were sitting on a blanket which she always brought to the games and put behind our team's bench. We were the only La Bar fans except for two guys who were lovers of the center fielder and the third baseman. The shore team had a few more fans who sat on blankets behind their team. I made the assumption that they were also boyfriends of the players.

"This game is too quiet. It's giving me the creeps," Diane said. "There aren't any young boys on bikes or old men watching."

"Perhaps that is why the police car hasn't come around yet," I said.

"It mustn't be 'officer hunky' in the car down there. If it were, he'd be up here."

"And you would be asking him for that date."

"Yeah, sure," she said sarcastically.

"I'd like to see what this guy looks like. If he's anything like what you and the guys have described, I might just ask him for a date myself."

Diane looked at me with a smirk. "Cee Jay, you never cease to amaze me."

George threw three strikes to put out the first hitter at the top of the fifth inning. The second hitter in the Asbury

Park rotation was a tall, lean guy who looked as though he might be better suited to run track than hit a baseball. His cap could not conceal his long blonde straight hair. In his white uniform, he seemed an innocent, young angel of twenty-one or two. He paused to take three or four swings of his bat before tapping in at home plate. His demeanor and stance projected an image of a man determined on hitting a home run.

And then, instantly, there was a cracking sound, more like a thump.

Everyone jumped up as George collapsed onto the mound.

I turned to look at Diane, but she was gone. She was already running toward the police car at the corner of the park.

Shock caused me to remain silently in place. I saw Diane running, I saw Paul screaming and running toward George, I saw the players forming a circle around the mound, and I saw the player, whom I had a moment ago thought looked like an angel at home plate, fall to his knees. By the time I got to the pitcher's mound, I saw that the police car had turned around and caught up with Diane; immediately the car's siren began wailing and the lights flashing.

I saw Paul sitting on the ground with his lover's head in his lap. Blood was covering George's face and Paul's hands; tears were streaming down his cheeks. The players who were all in their own private moments of shock knew that I was a friend and made a path for me to kneel beside George and Paul. I put my arm on Paul's shoulder and could feel his shaking body against mine. George was still, his lips never moved, blood was covering most of his ashen face. I blurted the only thing I was capable of saying, "Help is on the way."

Diane left the police car door open as she jumped out and ran toward us. The policeman was immediately behind her. Even in that moment I realized that he must be the attractive cop the three of them had been talking about earlier. He knelt down and started to checks George's vital signs. He looked up at the three of us. I detected compassion on his face. His first words were: "I've already called for an ambulance. It should be here right away."

As soon as he had finished speaking, the sirens of the ambulance could be heard. The municipal plaza in Bloomfield is just across from the park. The plaza consists of the city hall and court and police station on one side and the main library on the other. The police station had an EMT team and ambulance on the ready for any police emergency.

Paul relinquished his hold on George's head to the EMT guys who immediately put George's limp body on a stretcher. One of them put a mask, which was attached to a tank, over George's face. The other medic turned to Paul and asked if he wanted to ride in the ambulance with the victim. Paul immediately grabbed George's hand and helped place his lover in the ambulance and then jumped in with one of the EMT men. As the driver was closing the door, he yelled to the policeman. "Joel, we're taking him to Mountainside. See you in ER in a few." Immediately, the ambulance lights and siren were activated as it sped across the park onto Bloomfield Avenue.

The policeman was talking to the player who hit the ball. The Asbury Park player was still kneeling at home plate. He was sobbing now and seemed to be shivering and gasping for breath. As Diane and I approached the policeman, he touched the player's shoulder and said, "It's okay, Angel. It wasn't your fault. It was just a fucking line drive." He gave the player what appeared to be a card and added, "Call me, if you need me for anything." He then turned to us. "Are you friends of the victim?"

"Yes. We both live in the same building with George and Paul in Manhattan."

"Good. I need to get your names, et cetera for my report. They have taken him to Mountainside, which is the closest hospital. If you would like, you both can ride in my car up there."

"You go with him, Cee Jay. I'll get everything in my car and talk to some of the guys and then meet you at the hospital in just a few minutes."

I expected the policeman, who probably saw tragedy often on his job, to act in a calm, cool, collected and professional manner; but Diane surprised me. Her first reactions upon hearing the crack of the bat, running for help instantly, and now her manner in saying that she'd join us after a while seemed odd. She knew George and Paul far longer and was much closer to both of them than me. I was a nervous wreck, whereas Diane seemed very matter of fact.

As soon as we were in the police car, the officer wrote down a few notations and then stared ahead blankly without speaking. He rested his fist on his chin as though he was thinking of something.

"You know he's dead," he said softly turning to face me.

I could not fully grasp the implication of his words. "What do you mean 'he's dead'?" I muttered.

"You can't get a direct hit to the temple that hard and survive. It's actually worse than being shot with a bullet. I'm pretty sure he died instantly." He then started the car, but did not turn on his lights or siren. "There was no pulse when I checked. I'm willing to bet that his friend ... I think you said his name was Paul...realized it too. The hospital will report that he was dead on arrival there."

It all had happened so quickly that I could not accept the reality of George's death. Just a few minutes ago he was a healthy, active, fun loving twenty-seven year old lawyer playing his favorite sport, and now this cop is telling me he was dead. ... Old people die. ...Sick people die. ...Not beautiful, athletic men, playing a game. ...Soldiers may die in a foreign field, but why George in a god damn baseball field in god damn Bloomfield, New Jersey. No good God would ever let something like this happen. ...My emotions welled; I could not speak.

"He was George Miller, wasn't he?" the cop said to me after a long pause. "We both graduated high school the same year. I went to West Side High and George went to St. Benedict's, also in Newark. I remember our schools played a few football and baseball games against one another and George and I both played football and baseball. He was one hell of a good quarterback. I read the paper's write-ups of him getting full scholarships in both sports. I kept all the papers that had anything about sports when I was in high school. I could never figure out why he chose Wisconsin over Rutgers." He paused. "By the way, my name's Joel Freedman."

We shook hands as I told him my name.

"Last year when the department needed guys to cover your league games, I volunteered because I needed the extra money. I'm working on a master's in psychology at Rutgers. When I can schedule it, I play on the Bloomfield police baseball team. I'm a pitcher also. We cops also have a league. Boy, I have to admit that I was pretty surprised to see George Miller pitching for a gay team from New York." Again, Joel Freedman paused before choosing his words. "I assume he and Paul were lovers. Paul took the accident very poorly." I was surprised to hear a policeman use the word 'lover' so casually and with no hesitation. For me, it was comforting.

"Yes, they met playing baseball at Rutgers. George transferred to Rutgers in his sophomore year and moved to New York when he got a job working as a lawyer for the American Civil Liberties Union. Paul moved to New York the following year, and they have been together ever since."

"He's going to take his loss very hard, poor guy. I'm sure you will help him through all this."

"Yes. Diane and I will do what we can. She has known them longer than I."

We had arrived at the emergency entrance to Mountainside Hospital. In the waiting room, I found Paul sitting in a corner chair seemingly in a daze. He stood up as soon as he saw me and we hugged one another tightly. He was sobbing. George's blood was still on parts of his face, hands, and uniform.

"He's dead!" Paul yelled above his sobs. "Cee Jay, my George is dead. Can you believe it? God dam it, Cee Jay, my man is dead! ...How? Why?... I don't understand it. The doctors said he had something called an epidural hemorrhage... whatever the hell that is… and severe brain contusions, and a fractured skull. They said he died without knowing what hit him." We both sat down and I continued to hold him around the shoulders.

When we entered the hospital emergency area, the policeman went directly to the nurse at the desk. He now came over to us. He cuddled Paul's hand in his own. "I am very sorry for your loss today, Paul. I know that you and George loved one another very much. He was taken from you by a vicious line drive, a pitcher's worst nightmare." He turned to pull up a chair to face Paul directly.

"Irony of ironies," I said to Paul, "Joel here was a pitcher also and played against George in high school."

Joel smiled. "I hate to do this now," he said. "But I need to ask you a few questions. Okay?"

Paul nodded his assent.

"Good. First off, would you please spell your last name for me?" Paul obliged. "Thank you, Paul. Now may I have your address?" Again, Paul told the officer our street and his apartment number. "Thanks for that. Now may I have your telephone number? I may need to get in touch with you for some reason." Paul got confused and suddenly could not remember his area code and got some of the numbers confused, so I went over it again correctly for Joel to write it down.

"Now, for a few tougher questions. Does the name 'Angel Martinez' mean anything to you?"

Paul thought for a moment, and then said that he didn't know anybody by that name. "Why, …why do you ask?"

"That's the name of the fellow who hit the line drive. Had you ever seen him before?" Again, Paul responded in the negative. "Do you have any reason to believe that George may have known him?" I thought it ironic that his name was Angel because of my first impression when I saw him at the plate.

"No, I don't think so. …Why are you asking me about the son of a bitch who killed my lover?"

The policeman thought for a moment. It was as though he was reacting to Paul's statement. "I just need to be sure that it was 100% an accident." He paused again. "By the way, Angel Martinez was very dramatized by it also. Please don't have it in your heart to blame the kid. Can we all agree that it was purely a freakish accident?" He paused.

"Do you know where George's family lives and their telephone number?"

Paul hesitated for a long time before responding. He started crying again. "All I know is that his father died about four years ago. His mother lives in Bayonne with one of George's younger brothers. Beyond that, I don't know anything about his family. Ever since he told them about us, they pretty much have ignored him. Last time he saw his mother was on Christmas, and then only for a few hours. She insisted that he go to a catholic mass with her."

"We'll try to locate her," Joel said. "If my department can locate a phone number, I will call her today myself. The family will have to make arrangements for his funeral."

"He told me a few times that he wanted to be cremated and have his ashes scattered from the mound in Yankee Stadium," Paul blurted.

The policeman smiled, thought for moment, and then replied, "We'll see what we can do."

It was at that moment that Diane came into the waiting room. She and Paul immediately embraced. "You got to be brave, honey," was all she could say.

"He's dead, Diane. My dip shit lover is dead," Paul said aloud. "Killed by a god damn line drive to his head."

"I know, baby. I know." She continued to pat him on the back and then kissed him on the side of his face that didn't have blood. "Let's go home now and get you cleaned up. You got to be brave, honey. George would want you to be brave." She pulled him away and they both looked sadly into one another's eyes. She ran her hand over the side of his face that had George's blood the way a mother would if her child had been injured.

Lead by the policeman, the four of us silently left the waiting room. Before saying goodbye to us outside the hospital, the policeman gave each of us one of his cards. "Don't hesitate to call me if any of you have questions…. or just want to talk," Joel said.

I looked at the card before putting it in my pocket. In blue it read: 'Joel Freedman, Bloomfield Police Department, Community Outreach Counselor.'

None of us spoke much all the way back to Greenwich Village. I did notice that tears welled a few times in Diane's eyes, but she quickly wiped them away with her hand. I knew that she was fighting to remain brave for Paul's sake. She had to remain brave for herself. I am certain that as we drove home, the three of us realized that we would always associate April with that crack of the bat.

Chapter Nine

WHAT I LEARNED ABOUT JAMIE

It was a hot afternoon in mid-August. The temperature was around 95 degrees in the shade, but the humidity was unbearable. After trying to read in my small apartment that didn't have air conditioning, I decided to go to the bar where I knew it would be at least cooler.

"Hey, how's my big man from Jorsy?" Jamie Roberts was already in the bar and greeted me with his usual 'tough guy' from New Jersey fake impression.

"I'm hot, Jamie."

"Yeah, man, you sure is hot." Jamie emphasized the word *hot* in his snarky response. "Boy, you should get out of this heat and head down to the Jorsy shore."

"You're right there, Jamie," I said. "If I didn't have a test on Monday I might just have done that."

"You know I've never been to the Jorsy shore. Other than once when a john took me to Newark, I've never even been anywhere in the ol' Garden State. Where do you usually go, Atlantic City?" He took a deep gulp of his beer.

"No, I usually go to Asbury Park. It's much closer and the bus fare there is a lot less. It's the same Atlantic Ocean water and there is a boardwalk too."

"Hey, you and I should go there sometime," Jamie said.

"Jamie, you know that I don't pay for the chance to take a handsome young man such as yourself on a date."

"Seriously, Cee Jay, I'd like going to- what was it you called it- Asbury Park?- with you. It wouldn't be a date or anything. I'd even pay my own way. I'm serious, man. I'd like to see the Jorsy shore I hear so much about. All the bar faggots go to Jones Beach or out to Fire Island, but I don't like getting pine needles up my ass, ya know what I mean. Besides, I know that with you there's no pressure." Jamie took another swig on his beer. "So, what do ya say, let's go to Asbury Park."

I had not been to the New Jersey shore all summer and was anxious to get away from the Village, even if it were for a day, so I agreed to have Jamie accompany me to Asbury Park the following Saturday. It would be fun to get away from reading, schedules, classes, and study groups even if it were for a day. Jamie Roberts certainly would be different company for me also. He was gutsy, raw, crude, and different. Against the intellectual snobs I cavorted with at NYU, this country bumpkin was the perfect antidote.

We agreed to meet at the foot of the escalators in the Port Authority Bus Terminal on Eighth Avenue at 8:00 a.m. the following week. I gave him my card with my telephone number on it, just in case he had an all-nighter the Friday before or it ended-up raining on our parade. I think it was Mark Twain who once said: "If you don't like the weather in New Jersey, wait five minutes; it will change." In Jamie's case, however, it was not the weather I was afraid of changing. I fully expected him to cancel early Saturday morning because he was hung over from the night before, or still with one of his 'dates,' or- knowing Jamie- he might just forget about it and not show up at the Port Authority.

I arrived at the bus terminal a few minutes before eight, fully expecting not to see Jamie there; but he was there wearing his cut-off tattered jeans and his red cap- turned backwards, of course. He was carrying a gym bag in which he told me were his beach towel, bathing suit, sandals, and sun lotion. I wondered what the sun lotion would do to his facial pimples.

To make sure that he really meant paying his own way, I got in the ticket line before him and bought one round-trip ticket for myself and then stepped aside while Jamie did the same. As we walked to the platform and boarding the bus, we may have looked like a father-son pair, except that he was taller than me.

During the bus trip to Asbury Park, I learned a few things about him. For one, he had never been in the Lincoln Tunnel before. He thought the view of the Manhattan skyline from the top of the S-3 ramp was spectacular. "Boy, I wish I had a camera," Jamie enthused. "That's the Statue of Liberty!" I chuckled, thinking of the line from *Midnight Cowboy* where Joe Buck, a character in the film, gets a disparaging response to his question concerning our lady of Bedloe's Island.

When we passed the Meadowlands Sports Complex, I pointed out the football stadium to him. "Gosh!" Jamie exclaimed. "I didn't know the Giants didn't play in New York. Why are they called the New York Giants when they're here in New Jersey?" That, I told him was a mystery to all the people of New Jersey. I explained that it was probably because this area is technically known as Secaucus and New York sounds better than Secaucus. The whole area around the complex used to be a big swamp and the actual area of the Meadowlands was known for raising and killing pigs when I was a boy. I told him that the smell of the pigs was so strong that you could smell it clear across the Passaic River into Newark when the wind was right.

He seemed to be generally interested in whatever I told him. As we rode, I noticed that he dropped the tough guy affectation and starting saying 'New Jersey' rather than "Jorsy." His boyish mannerism seemed more genuine, and I was actually beginning to like Jamie Roberts in his new environment. I didn't feel as self- conscious about his being with me.

Asbury Park in the early sixties was still a very nice shore resort. On Easter Sundays it was New Jersey's answer to the Easter Parade around St. Patrick's Cathedral on Fifth Avenue of New York. People from all over the state would either drive or take buses to walk the Boardwalk. The ladies proudly wore their new hats and the men, who held their wives or girlfriends by the arm, were proud of their new two or three-breasted suits and wide neon ties. Most men wore felt hats on the Boardwalk on Easter Sunday. The water was too cold for swimming, but a few shoeless youngsters could always be seen flying kites on the beach. Hundreds of people would stroll along the boardwalk from the Paramount Theater Arcade to the Casino on the southern side. In those days the big hotel was the elite Carlton across from the Paramount. A new motel, the Empress, was right on the boardwalk and offered ocean-view rooms. Smaller hotels, guest houses, and bed-and-breakfasts were spread throughout the beach area. All had well- manicured front lawns and big porches with rocking chairs. Nearly all of them were covered with geranium pots. Memorial Day through Labor Day was considered 'the season' and without a reservation, it was hard to find a room for the night.

It was said in certain social groups of the sixties that Asbury Park was controlled by the 'gay mafia.' I had no proof of this claim except that I did know at least one hotel and one motel that catered only to gay men. There were two restaurants that were frequented exclusively by the homosexual crowd. There may have been more, but I knew of one so-called leather or biker bar, two discos, and three regular gay bars all within a few blocks of one another. During the summer season it was not unusual to see male couples and groups of men cavorting together on the beach. There was no nudity or vulgar language; there certainly was no drinking of alcohol, and drugs were practically unknown on the Asbury Park beach. In general the gays behaved in a manner so mild that I often felt that the straights and family groups around them probably had no idea what or whom they were surrounded by. I suppose the old expression that you had to be one to know one, applied here.

As a teenager, who was admittedly wet-behind-the-ears, I remember being propositioned by a life guard in the showers of the men's bathhouse across the street from the beach. It was six o'clock and the place was about to close. We were the only two in the bathhouse on that particular weekday. The life guard volunteered to soap up my back if I would do the same for him. I could not help but to notice that he had an erection which he was massaging and seemingly very proud of. When he got the message that I was not interested in playing in the shower with him, he quickly left the outdoor shower area and disappeared into his own cabana in the complex. When he left, I thought about the 'big-man on-campus' reputation this guy must have had at his college. Many college students worked during the summers as life guards. This one was certainly beautifully tanned, well-built and handsome; he was probably very popular with the co-eds. But I would not be surprised to learn that he later turned out to be a pedophile.

Jamie and I changed into our bathing suits in that same bathhouse and crossed the street to the beach. He picked out a spot for us and put his big towel down. I could tell that he was checking out the area as he patted his towel smooth in the sand. "Hell, Cee Jay, you never told me there'd be so many queers in Asbury Park," he exclaimed.

"It takes one to know one, Jamie," I said. "Most people around here would not know that they were in Jorsy's answer to Fire Island." I deliberately accented 'Jorsy' for his delight.

Today, Asbury Park is a different place from the one Jamie and I visited that August. Unfortunately, the racial riots that took place in Newark affected the decline of New Jersey's popular, central beach resort. Several factors led to Asbury's demise, including a population shift. Johnny Cash, who invested in an attempt to renovate the Carlton Hotel, lost millions. Many homes, businesses, and hotels were shuttered and burned. A large condominium complex was torched just as it was being completed. Drugs were introduced into the area, resulting in a huge crime increase. The homosexual population deserted the city. Those who could afford to, bought old, Victorian style homes in the bordering town of Ocean Grove and turned them into fashionable bed- and- breakfast inns. The town that jeeringly was referred to as 'Ocean Grave' is now competing with Cape May to its south for the tourists' money. A similar shift in gentrification generated by gays can be seen in Jersey City, New Jersey; South Beach, Florida; and, of course, San Francisco, California.

Jamie and I went in the water and did the usual frolicking around that two men might do. I was surprised to learn that Jamie was a really good swimmer. I thought to myself that he was a different person from the one I knew at La Bar. At one point he swam out beyond the breakers and I saw and heard the life guards whistling and motioning to him to get back to the beach. I wondered if any of those life guards would try to seduce Jamie or anyone younger in the bathhouse showers. These life guards seemed more professional and older to me, however.

When Jamie came in, we walked up to our beach towels. I was surprised when he asked if I would put some sun lotion on his back. He was naturally very pale, and I noticed that he had pimples on his back as well as his face. He lay on his stomach and propped his head over his arms. I poured a substantial amount of lotion on his back and rigorously started spreading it. I squeezed his shoulders in a playful manner as if I were giving him a massage. He moaned in appreciation of how good that felt. I noticed that Jamie did have a nice, round ass. As a result, the speedo-style bathing suit he wore did seem appropriate. When I squished some lower on the upper portion of his legs and worked up to his ass and crouch area, he let out a "Watch it, Jorsy man! There are kids on this beach! Don't start something you can't finish." I laughed. He turned around and looked at me calmly.

"Do you want me to do you?" Jamie asked.

"That depends on what you mean by 'do me,'" I said.

"Don't get smart."

I sat on the towel with my legs crossed. "Okay," I said, "you can do me, but be gentle with me." I don't know why it popped into my mind at that moment; but it did, and I repeated the famous line from *Tea and Sympathy*: "In the future when you think back on this moment, and you will, be kind."

Jamie slapped me across the back. "Okay, Deborah. You ol' drama queen!" I was shocked to realize that Jamie made the connection and knew that Deborah Kerr played the lead in that movie.

Maybe, Jamie, is more intelligent than I give him credit for, I thought.

Jamie Roberts stopped rubbing but kept his hand still on my back. He was silent. "Is something wrong?" I asked.

"I was just thinking," Jamie said. "You and me should get together sometime. You know, do it. I would really….." He paused. "I would really like to spend a night with you. Alone! … I like you a lot, Cee Jay, ….. just in case you didn't know…. There, I've said it."

There was silence before he continued rubbing the sun tan lotion on my back. I didn't know how to respond. Here was a kid that I didn't particularly like, a kid who seemed to be making a living by prostituting himself, a kid whom I didn't consider attractive, opening himself to me that way. I thought of him as a kid, even though he was only a few years younger than myself. After a moment's hesitation, I reached my arm behind my back and grabbed his hand. I said the only thing I could think of at the moment: "Thank you, Jamie. That's very sweet of you. I guess we'll both have to see what happens. Okay?"

Finished with the lubrication, Jamie capped the bottle and turned on his side facing me. He seemed to be very pensive.

"What?" I said after a while.

"I'm going to tell you something that no one else knows about me. None of the guys at the bar really know me. But I want you to know, Cee Jay."

"Okay." I said this as half a question and half a way of saying 'go on…' "What is Jamie Roberts' big secret?"

"I'm married!"

"You are!" I said half questioning and half in amazement.

"Yeah, I've been married for three years. Melissa and I got married right after high school. We dated for two years in high school in West Virginia. She was pregnant at the time we graduated, and she couldn't tell her parents because they did not like me, so we eloped and came to New York. I actually live in Brooklyn."

"Hold on here a minute, Jamie. You're telling me that you are married for three years and have a baby and you live in Brooklyn. I don't get it. You hang out almost every night in a gay bar in the Village, you have sex with men as a prostitute, and a minute ago you practically told me that you are in love with me. Now you're telling me that you are straight and happily married with a child. What gives with you, dude?"

"I know it's weird, ain't it."

"Weird isn't the word for it. Crazy, maybe," I said.

"Yeah, it is crazy," Jamie admitted. "Maybe I am crazy, but it's the truth. I thought you'd understand. And if we're to be friends, you should know this about me. I've told Melissa about you and she knows I'm here with you. I've told her a lot about you; she knows how I feel about you."

"Does she know that you hustle out of a gay bar several times a week?"

"Yeah, she knows. She ain't happy about it, but she knows. I'm bi-sexual, Cee Jay." He paused. "Do you know what that means?"

I must admit that back in the early 60's the term was seldom used among ordinary people. I had a vague intellectual idea what the term meant but never really had met anyone who told me he or she was bisexual. Perhaps in the decade before the word *homosexual* was just as analytical. In a way, Jamie's giving me this revelation, caused me to study my own psyche. "Yes, I know what the word means, but honestly you are the first person I have ever met who has at least admitted openly that he is bisexual."

"The truth of the matter is that I'm not so 'open,' as you say. Melissa knew I was bisexual after our third date as juniors in high school, but not too many people know. My parents don't know, her parents don't know….anyway her old man may, but I'm not sure. None of my friends back in West Virginia know. Our landlord, neighbors, not even my pastor at church know I swing both ways."

Suddenly, this jerky kid in front of me became a whole new person with a life story that topped any I had ever heard.

"The relationship I have with my wife Melissa is very good. She is my wife and best friend. We still have great sex together about two times a week." Jamie smiled sheepishly. "I guess I have a high testosterone level. When I'm with guys, I'm very cautious. I go for a check- up when I suspect something, but so far I've been lucky. I did get the crabs once, but got clean before doing anything with anyone else. The truth is that I do hustle, but I don't make much money doing it because I don't hook up with the kind of guys I want to that often. Most of the ones I do hook up with don't have that much money anyway.

"Melissa works at home as a typist. She's a very good, fast typist. And I work four hours a day, six days a week as a sexton at my church. Father O'Hearn is a good man, but I'm sure if he knew I was also half-gay and a hustler, he'd fire me. He baptized my little girl, Barbara. So with Melissa's typing job, my working at the church, and a little on the side hustling, we don't live high, but we get by and are happy. If Melissa becomes pregnant again, we might have some problems, but we are both careful about that."

"Wow! You're blowing my mind, Jamie."

"Here, I want to show you some pictures." From his gym bag he produced a photo album. "This is Melissa," he said passing the wallet- sized album to me. Melissa was very beautiful; she had long blonde hair that looked natural; and her smile was genuine. She was standing in what appeared to be a backyard in the country; she was wearing a gown and could have passed as a model.

"She's very beautiful," I said. "Where was this picture taken?"

"That was in her backyard down in West Virginia at her sister's wedding about five months ago; Melissa was the maid of honor."

He turned a few pages before handing the photo album back to me. "This is my little bundle of joy. Her name's Barbara, after my wife's mother." The picture was of Jamie with a beautiful baby girl in his lap. He was playing with her little fingers. "She's my little Barbie doll."

He paused. "I think women can handle a husband's being bisexual better than a man can," Jamie said. "Melissa knows that I will always love her and Barbara, but I need to have sex with guys once in a while too. Melissa is the one and only female I ever made it with. I have no desire to have sex with any other woman. She's all I need that way."

"Do you ever have sex with men that are not johns?" I asked.

"A few times, years ago, when I was just coming out but not since. Probably, if I had met the right guy before I started dating Melissa, I would be attached to him the way I am with her. But gay love is hard to come by, Cee Jay. And if I can't have love, I'll do it for the money because I like doing it with men and I almost feel that I have to at times; but every guy I make it with I keep hoping will show me the kind of love and understanding I am looking for. Most men that I am attracted to only want sex. I want sex and love. Money is just extra. Yeah, I dream someday of raising a family in a big house with a white picket fence. Yeah, I definitely want that all- American dream. I guess that's never going to happen with me and a gay guy."

Jamie's confession- if that was what it was- was overwhelming. I had enough of playing the priest or psychoanalyst for one afternoon and suggested that we get something to eat and drink on the boardwalk before catching the six o'clock bus back to Manhattan. His story had hit a tight string with me. It made me feel raw and vulnerable in my own feelings toward my own sexuality. Perhaps his story was close to my own.

As we were changing out of our bathing suits, I asked Jamie what type of guys he liked.

"Guys like you, Cee Jay," was his answer.

Chapter Ten

HERMAN AUGSTORFER

The excitement of change and renewal which was affecting so many aspects of American life during the 1960's also affected education. New ideas on how to educate children in the twentieth century were emerging out of places like Teachers' College, Columbia University and Harvard School of Education and others. The new gurus of education were not necessarily classroom teachers, but they had ideas on how to do it and created "buzz words" that were to alter the course of learning for decades. The adage: "Those that can, do; those that can't, teach; and those that can't teach, teach teachers how to teach; and those that can't teach teachers, become administrators" took on real meaning in the second half of the century.

Among the many buzz words relating to the teaching of English during the '60's was "contemporary literature." In order to be a forerunner in this curriculum, NYU was offering a graduate course by this name, and I was enrolled in the class. The goal was two-fold: First, to improve reading on the secondary level by offering students a study of more current literature, rather than the usual fare generally taught; and second, to create a greater interest in reading by presenting issues which were relative to students.

When we consider the literature which was presented in most high schools through the '50's, a change was obviously necessary. A typical English curriculum would include:

Freshman year: ***Silas Marner*** or ***Animal Farm*** and ***Romeo and Juliet***

Sophomore year: ***The Miracle Worker*** or ***The Diary of Anne Frank*** and ***Julius*** Caesar

Junior year: ***Our Town*** or ***The Red Badge of Courage*** and ***Macbeth***

Senior year: ***Pride and Prejudice*** and ***Hamlet*** or ***King Lear***

We may consider whether reading Shakespeare ever led to reading improvement. The fault of such limitations in the choice of literature was not always the fault of teachers who found it perhaps easier to teach and grade formal grammar. Often the standard textbooks only included these selections, and school boards could not afford paying for additional books, including paperbacks, which was a relatively new concept in the early '60s. Another major limitation on literary selections was (and perhaps still is) community and religious control as well as parental concerns.

I myself had been involved in having to defend the teaching of such seemingly innocuous books as ***Flowers for Algernon*** and ***The Grapes of Wrath*** before administrators and boards of education, even though those school leaders admitted that they personally had not read these books. However, once a parent found a line or two that was not in keeping with white, Anglo Saxon, Christian principles, it was the Scopes-Monkey trial redux. Yet, for some reason the same people who objected to rather innocent passages in these books did not oppose their innocent, little darlings from studying a story in which two under-age teens meet at a party, fall instantly in love, elope, and consummate the "marriage" within a 48- hour time span- all within a framework of street violence, killing and suicide. While millions of teens have read ***Romeo and Juliet*** as standard fare in school, other great works such as ***Huckleberry Finn*** were banned because of "inappropriate language."

As a member of the Contemporary Literature class, I was assigned to a committee that was to go into the field to actually study what was being taught in English classes in the high schools of New York. Our goal was to eventually write an article for the prestigious ***English Journal.*** I was given the task of investigating a high school in the upper west side of Manhattan that had a course actually entitled "contemporary literature."

I contacted the school, and in a brief conversation with the principal arranged to meet with the teacher and observe a class or two the following week.

Upon arriving at the school, I went to the principal's office. The principal was a handsome man who seemed to be in his early thirties. He was tall, had crew-cut hair, and was well built. He was the type you immediately thought played football in college and coached high school for a few years while teaching and working on an advanced degree in administration. He was friendly and welcomed me into his office to talk for a few minutes before a student would escort me to the class.

Principal John Davis had no hesitation in letting me know that he was not particularly a fan of the teacher, Mr. Herman Augsdorfer, or his contemporary literature class which was a "singleton" elective, meaning that it was a new class that met just once a day. Mr. Augsdorfer taught five other classes and in order to teach contemporary literature had to be taken from his extra-duty assignment, which was a study hall. Augsdorfer had applied for and was given a National Council of Arts grant to teach the elective, which resulted in many scheduling "headaches" for Principal Davis and the guidance department. Davis explained that originally 50 of the best students in school signed up for the course, but Augsdorfer "cleverly" stipulated in his grant proposal that the class should not have more than twenty-five students because of the extra amount of writing the students would be required to do. These good students, not only did not have time in their schedules for study halls, but might have to drop other, older electives. There was also the problem of what period this elective would be taught because it might conflict with other, required courses the students might have. "To make matter even worse," Davis explained, "Augsdorfer's grant permitted any student in any grade to elect this class. I have a counselor for freshmen and sophomores and another one who only schedules junior and seniors. Because of our lunch schedules, this knocked out two possible periods when it could be held.

"You can imagine the hell of a scheduling problem this became for my guidance people," principal Davis continued. "Of the fifty youngsters who signed up for the class, we could only free up twenty for this class. And I had to beg one of my coaches to take over Augsdorfer's study hall. Then Augsdorfer gave his class a reading list and a syllabus on the first day of class; and the next day, three students wanted out. If you want my opinion, Mr. Seton, this class was just too much trouble for the seventeen youngsters now enrolled in it. Besides, all of them are already in our Regent's English classes. We have 2,400 hundred in this building, Mr. Seton. We just can't accommodate a few who may respond to one teacher's idea for new approaches, grant or no grant. I hope you can understand the problem here."

He paused momentarily. "Augsdorfer is not a popular teacher," he said. "He fails at least two students per class. If any of these 17 bright students fail his elective, we'll have a hell of a time with their parents when it comes time to send records to colleges."

Just then the bell rang and Davis escorted me to his outer office and introduced me to a student who was waiting to show me to Mr. Augsdorfer's contemporary literature class. The halls were crowded and noisy, but as we managed to go up the two floors to the class, the student guide told me that he would have liked to be in the contemporary literature elective, but felt the work load was too great because he had football practice every day and was having difficulty keeping up with his required courses. We arrived at room 306 just as the bell signaling the beginning of the next class rang. My guide introduced me to Mr. Augsdorfer who was waiting to the door. I shook hands with the teacher and then with the student who quickly took off down the hall. As he closed the door, the teacher suggested that I take a seat in the back of the room.

As I walked to the back of the room, the teacher briefly introduced me to the class as a graduate student at New York University. The students gave me a quick look and then immediately proceeded to fumble in their pile of books for a black and white hardcover notebook. "The topic for today's writing is on the board. You will have the usual ten minutes. Date your entry and begin." Augsdorfer's pronouncement seemed to be routine; the class quickly began writing in the composition notebooks.

Before class the teacher had written on the blackboard the topic: "What new element(s) of Existentialism did you find in the two assigned chapters for today? Explain fully."

I made note of the way the teacher immediately began class with a writing exercise, which was apparently standard. It was then that he quickly scanned the room and completed a paper which I assumed was an attendance form which he slid into the frame of the door. This too was also part of the routine of his classroom. He then walked to the back of the room.

The class is reading Albert Camus' ***The Stranger,"*** he said to me. "Before I distributed the books, I gave them a list of fourteen characteristics of Existentialism, which I briefly explained. Their job is to analyze the novel in light of these characteristics. The assignment for today was to read chapters one and two of part two, so we are about half way through the novel."

"Do you always begin class by having the students do some writing?" I asked.

"Yes. In many classes the students don't do any writing. In mine, they always have ten minutes of the period to write. A few teachers permit the students to write on anything, but I always have a directed topic. It keeps them on their toes and gives me the opportunity to do the housekeeping chores."

He returned to the front of the room. After a quick study of the room, he said, "Any problems, questions?" A girl raised her hand, and Augsdorfer went to her and quietly discussed something with her. He then moved to another student who seemed to be finished writing. Whatever he said to the boy, must have been encouraging because the young man immediately opened his notebook and began writing again.

While the students continued to write, I took notice of the teacher. Augsdorfer seemed to be in his late thirties or early forties. His black hair was prematurely graying. His beard made him, I felt, appear older than he probably was. His wire-framed glasses were round. He seemed to be about five feet, six or seven and was a little heavy around the stomach and waist; I judged him to weigh about 180. He was modestly dressed in a long-sleeve white shirt with a gray bow tie with little black dots, a gray cardigan sweater, dark blue pants. In all, he could well pass as a college professor rather than a high school teacher. With his demeanor, appearance, and name, he may have even been taken for a rabbi if he wore a yarmulke to class.

"You might like to see these," he said handing me a course syllabus and a typewritten lesson plan for today's class. "You may keep them," he said as he turned away and slowly walked back around the room to observe the progress of the writing assignment, He paused to look over the shoulders of some, to ask questions of others, or to answer a student's question.

I quickly scanned the syllabus. Listed as one of the books was Albert Camus' The Stranger, which I assumed was the novel currently under discussion. I quickly scanned the list of "required" and "suggested" readings. It was immediately obvious that by 'contemporary' literature, the instructor did not necessarily mean "published on or after 1960." I did, however, realize that most of the titles were not in most current anthologies used in public schools. They all did, however, relate to contemporary issues. Among those titles that were in Augsdorfer's syllabus were **Siddartha**, **The Grapes of Wrath**, **The Lord of the Flies, Animal Farm**, **A Separate Peace**, **1984, I Never Promised You a Rose Garden**, **Brave New World**, and **Catcher in the Rye**. One title which I found curious to be on the list of 'contemporary' works was Shakespeare's **Hamlet**. I made a mental note to ask the instructor about this later, but certainly all of the works cited would give me and my class back at NYU a wealth of material to discuss.

I did not ask for or even expect to receive a detailed lesson plan, but was grateful for it. I was not there to evaluate the teacher's abilities or methods, but even without looking at the lesson plan, in the eight or nine minutes I was in the classroom I had determined that the instructor was an intelligent, well-organized, no- nonsense, and thorough pedagogue. *Here is a teacher*, I thought, *that I would like to emulate.* I was particularly impressed that even though this was a literature class, he was able to incorporate meaningful writing skills into his lessons. It was evident that he made his students think creatively and express themselves orally.

He kept the stimulated discussion on topic. I noted that the students actually had more time talking than the teacher. Before the class ended, he had written the sixth characteristic on the chalk board: 'Detachment from spiritualism.' The assignment was also written on the board: 'Read the next 20 pages, 105 to 125.' I thought that the assignment of reading twenty pages of fiction did not seem overly demanding or challenging to junior and senior students, particularly those who were thinking of going to college. After pointing to the assignment and repeating it aloud, Herman said, "As you read tonight's assignment, try asking yourself if Meursault is insane or is he more like yourself than you would care to admit."

As the students left the room, I overheard a few of them joking about who was and who wasn't as psychotic as Meursault. Two of them stopped in front of the room to discuss something with Augsdorfer. When all the students left the room, I thanked the teacher for letting me observe the class. I told him that I truly thought it was an excellent class. I thanked him for the syllabus, including the list of readings, which would give my classmates and me I much to consider. As we walked out of the room together, I asked him why ***Hamlet*** was on the bibliography.

"It's simple," Augsdorfer said. "The play is a great classic, but it's not taught in any other class in our entire school because it is not in any anthology we use. I think it should be. And what could be more contemporary than issues such as incest, homosexuality, corruption, greed, and suicide?"

He smiled and winked at me. "And I hear it's going to be produced this coming season in 'Shakespeare in the Park' at the Delacort.

"I trust you can find your way out? He said. We shook hands, and I left him at the door to his next class.

On the way back to my apartment from my assistant teaching class, I decided to stop at La Bar. It was late in the afternoon, but too early for the after-five o'clock crowd to come in for 'Happy Hour' priced drinks, so I thought the place would be relatively quiet. I wanted to relax with a drink and then go home for dinner. It had been a week after my visit to the public high school and observing Herman Augstorfer's contemporary lit class.

I was sitting on a bar stool, when I noticed that Herman Augstorfer was at a bench up against the wall. He was engrossed in a newspaper, and had not seen me enter the bar from the side door. He had a large beer mug on the keg in front of him. As soon as Mario brought my martini, I got up to visit with the teacher.

"Hello, Mr. Augsdorfer. I'm glad to see you again." I sat down next to him on the bench without being invited.

The teacher looked up at me and removed his reading glasses. "Oh! Mr. …. Seton, isn't it? Surprise, surprise…. Running into you here."

I smiled. "I guess most of Manhattan comes into La Bar. Please call me Cee Jay."

"True. Very true. How are you doing at the University, Cee Jay? And I'm Herman. Okay."

"Fine. Thank you, fine. I'm glad we are meeting here. It saves me the trouble of writing a thank you letter. This way I can tell you in person how good it was to observe your class and learn about your grant proposal and to see it in progress. I hope the NCTE endorses it and encourages a very real need for change in our profession. At NYU my own contemporary lit class was enthusiastic as well as very impressed. My colleagues and I are still discussing your syllabus."

"Thank you. It's good to hear that people in academia are listening and trying to make the changes needed in the high school English curriculum."

I smiled. "When I first started teaching, I had all the ninth- grade classes in our school. The curriculum dictated that I spend exactly six weeks on Sir Walter Scott's *Ivanhoe.* The books had to be at least ten years old, and some board of education member back then must have felt that everyone must read this great novel because we had the standard, original version and a large-print, abridged version for all the 'slower' kids."

"I can't imagine spending six weeks on any one book," Herman said. "It must have been torture for those youngsters. I bet they hated it."

"I tried to keep them amused with the usual song and dance routines such as papier-mache projects of castles when I wasn't teaching the vocabulary or parsing sentences found in the book."

"I bet the other English teachers in your school were happy teaching the same book year after year that was assigned for their grade because once they had all the lesson plans done the first year, they never had to do any extra work to change them."

You're probably right about that, Herman."

"So tell me. What did your fellow students say about my choice of works? Did they question **Hamlet**, as you did?"

"No, Shakespeare wasn't a problem. Neither were **Catcher in the Rye** and **Death of a Salesman.** What really caused controversy were the Existential novels, particularly the one you were teaching when I visited your class."

"**The Stranger.**"

"Yes. I have no difficulty with high school students learning about Existentialism, but many of my peers thought that the concepts of this attitude toward life could be too upsetting and difficult for teenagers to correctly grasp. The idea of the meaninglessness of life, which you listed as a characteristic of the Existential philosophy, for example."

"mmm. After what The Third Reich did to my Jewish relatives at places like Auschwitz and what the US did in Hiroshima and is now doing in Vietnam, it's hard to believe that grad students might think that teenagers should not even consider this characteristic."

"I tend to agree with you about that, Herman. However, there is the characteristic of atheism to deal with. Have any parents complained yet that you may be teaching atheism?"

"Not yet, but I am expecting that shoe to fall. I'm not teaching atheism. I'm teaching 'about' atheism. It's like teaching about religion and preaching in favor of a specific religion. Atheism most definitely exists in the world today; and it does affect all of our attitudes whether we like it or not, so we should be aware of it. Our civilization no longer revolves around a God- centered universe as it did during the Middle Ages."

"Yes, but many people firmly believe in God. Many parents as well as their kids still believe in- and- tote their Bibles around, even if they never read them fully in context. Any change in religious belief is bound to face criticism."

I waited while Augdorfer took a long swallow of his draft. "It's all bullshit!" he exclaimed.

"What?" I was shocked to hear him use such language.

"Religion. I think organized religions as we know them, are bullshit." He paused. "I'm saying this to you, an intelligent professional in a friendly discussion. I'd never say it as directly to a student or his or her parents."

"Okay. You don't believe in religion per se. Then do you believe in God?'

"No."

"Oh, so you're an atheist?"

Augsdorfer smiled. "No, I am not an atheist."

"You just said that you do not believe in God and at the same time you deny being an atheist. Frankly, Herman, I'm confused."

"When you speak of '*God*,' what do you mean? Suppose we were to speak about a cure for cancer, what do you mean? Could I say I believe there is a cure for cancer? No, I couldn't. I would have to do more than merely believe there was a cure for the disease. Unless I knew definitively that there was a cure, it would do me no good. How can I possibly follow a religion, therefore, or believe in a God and eternity unless I knew more about it?"

"Well, then," I said, "you are an agnostic."

"Agnostic, atheist, label me as anything you please, if classification helps you. I think of myself as a realist." Herman took another drink of his beer. "Do you believe in or know this power you call God? I mean really believe in this thing…. This God…. About whom we all know so little?"

"I can merely conjecture at the power of a Divine Being through reason. Through what I do know, I am able to give Him certain attributes. It ultimately comes to basic belief, and I do believe in a Supreme Being or God."

He seemed sincerely interested as he took another swig of brew. "Good! Explain to me why you do."

"Well, I did have a course once in apologetics."

"I don't give a damn if you had apologetics and theology and were taught by Jesuits. I asked you why you believed in God, and I don't want a textbook answer either."

This time it was I that gulped the last of my alcohol. "Look," I started, "suppose you and I were the only persons left on earth Let's say there was a great plague that wiped out all human life but ours. We would stop to consider creation more seriously. We would look about us and see the great world, the atmosphere, continents, oceans, all parts of the harmonious whole. We would realize the vast universe: the sun, moon, stars, and planets. Then we would have to ask ourselves what all this universe would be if we, the last rational creatures, weren't here to realize it? Everything would become oblivion. The world, therefore, was created for man's appreciation as the only rational creature. Take man away from creation, and what is left of it? Nothing! Doesn't this prove, then, that man is the purpose or reason for creation? By definition 'purpose' means the reason for which something exists or is done. Here then, is the eternal in the purpose of a God. In the end view there can be but one reason for being and that is God."

Herman hesitated and then stood with his glass in hand. "I'm ready for a refill," he said.

I walked over to the bar with him.

The bartender was quick in refilling our glasses. Augstorfer used the bartender to begin his counter argument. "Mario, you studied biology in the college you went to, didn't you?"

"Yeah, I had a year of bio before I dropped out."

"Would you say that a one-celled amoeba seems to know its own environment quite well?"

"Yes, I believe it does. It knows enough to know where to move by actually changing its body. It knows about its own food and how to engulf it. An amoeba does seem to understand its own environment to get along quite well even to include multiplying itself. What do you want to know for?"

Cee Jay here tells me that man is the ultimate thing in creation. I'm telling him that man no more knows the universe then the amoeba his. Actually, in the total picture of the universe man may be as an amoeba in a drop of water."

Mario gave us both a strange look and walked away to wait on someone else. Herman continued our dialogue. "I am not denying the possibility of a God. As you said, I may be an agnostic. But isn't the very thought of one indeed almost incomprehensible by man?"

"No, I disagree. We can use our own reasoning to achieve certain conclusions. Consider now, God as the first cause-cause. Instead of referring to Him as God... a mere label...

let's consider this power as the 'cause- cause' of creation. Trace the history of man back to Adam and Eve. We have to ask where they came from. Ask the same question of every single thing on earth, and you realize that somewhere, somehow this chain had a beginning. Even if you traced all of creation back to one element, one atom, you could not proceed until another force, another element – did something to it. There had to be a beginning and this beginning, I believe, is God. Science calls it 'The Big Bang' without ever defining the cause of that 'Big Bang.'

"You are going around in circles. What you are saying is that God had no beginning. That He always was and always will be. This is as difficult to comprehend as there being two original elements that caused the Big Bang. Where did this force you call God come from? Why couldn't all of creation stem from two atoms as readily as from a personified deity?"

"Man has been made with the capacity to have a great mind and a soul. Try as we may, we cannot breathe a soul into an artificial brain. Since we have this element life- this soul- the person, force, or thing that made us must also possess it."

"You seem to be denying the fact that the pupil may become more learned than the teacher. You are also denying that the offspring may be more healthy, strong, wiser, and more intelligent than the parent. That the child's IQ could be greater. You deny the biological possibility of developing a better race by mating the super-specimens of a species. This whole idea of eugenics, I remind you, was tried by members of the Third Reich. Not even Charles Darwin, however, could predict a final end to evolution."

Herman's counter arguments had some elements which contained some worth- while thought and which I suppose should have continued in debate. Rather than belaboring any one point, however, I chose to introduce a new idea.

"Truly," I said you must attribute the order and design you observe in the universe to some Supreme Being. Take for example, such a simple item as a wrist watch. Look at all the fine, intricate parts that had to be put into it in such perfect order. Do you think that mere blind chance, a mere juggling of parts, could make a watch? Much greater than a watch is the perfection of the universe. Surely the elements that bind the earth and cause it to go around on its axis could not have formed themselves by mere chance."

"The order and design theories in theology are good. However," Herman continued, "let's pause and think about this. You mentioned the common wrist watch as an example. Granted, a watch is an instrument of precision. So is a cyclotron. But what does a watch do?"

"It tells time. Permits history."

"Exactly. Now what is time? Time- as you said permits history. It records the life and death of creatures. It tells us how the elements are reacting, day and night. Time moves on. Even when the world at the poles is in darkness for months, we can know how the earth is rotating by telling time, by using this device. Now why must there be day and night on this earth? The moon, as well as some planets, has a side that never has seen the light of the sun. How much design and order Is there in the birth of a deformed child, a cyclone, whirlpool, volcano, earthquake? You speak of order and design. What do we really know about order and design when all we have to compare it with is our own environment on earth, which we just accept as it is."

He continued. "Rather than giving a watch as an example, consider a herd of cattle. A stampede is something outside of order; it is not a design we would hope for. However, in a stampede of cattle, which animal or animals are out of order: the ones that continue the wild run or the one that stops short for some reason and is trample over as a result, this nonconformist? The chaos theory I believe applies here, Cee Jay."

With this last bit of 'philosophizing' for one day, I drained the last drop in my martini glass.

"This sure has been a strange conversation to have in a gay bar; but I've enjoyed talking to you, Herman." I extended a handshake.

"So why not? God's a good topic. A bit more erudite than most of the sports stories you usually hear in La Bar. Maybe the next time we meet here we can talk about politics." He hesitated. "Or unidentified flying objects. Now, that's a topic I'd really like talking about. I have a theory that it is related to God. Yes, let's talk UFOs, next time."

Chapter Eleven

TREVOR HILTON

After living in the city for over a year-and-a-half, having many visits to La Bar, a few 'intimate' talks with Paul, and a few 'intimate' relationship, I thought I knew all about the gay sex scene. Of course, knowing somethings and practicing the right thing are not always followed. I don't know if any of the 'right things' were followed when I met Trevor Hilton. Trevor was the first man that I believe I fell in love with.

One of the most fascinating aspects of going to La Bar was that one went there in hope of meeting 'Mr. Right.' There may be two hundred people in the bar, so you cruise around, and pick out one or two you would like to get to know. When you have the opportunity, you make the moves necessary for a connection.

It is a strange ritual, but what causes us to make these decisions of the heart- or the gonads- or what the hell else causes us to be attracted to another human being? What is it in us that reacts to the physical? Is it color of skin, color of eyes, hair? Is it clothes? Height? Weight? Hair style? Strange, but these very physical attributes are often used above all other aspects. Our minds have made the selection before we speak to one another, hear the sound of the other person's voice; this, I believe, is the second thing we look for in our cruising ritual. We want to connect on a verbal level. Perhaps this is our reason for using such innocuous lines as 'Do you come here often? … Pretty cold out there tonight" or …nice jacket you're wearing.' Some more daring guys may be more direct: "Hi, my name is Buddy. What's yours?" This last opener usually involves a handshake. No matter what opening line we use, isn't it really the verbal response that becomes our second basis of judgement? The nature and tone of the response, often determines what we do next. If the response is something like "Hi, I'm not interested" or "Sorry, I'm with my boyfriend over there" or the person has a high pitched squeaky voice that immediately grates on you, the tendency might be to move away silently while thinking: *Fuck you, asshole!"*

The Third step in the cruising ritual is the manner of that response. Did the guy seem glad you spoke to him? Did the response give you an opportunity to continue talking? The initial bit of conversation is very telling. It may indicate that your new number has a sense of humor, is drunk, depressed or has a positive outlook, etc.

One thing I quickly found out for myself was: Never keep the conversation going longer than fifteen minutes before making damn sure it's going to lead to a real date or sex. If the guy just wants to talk about his wonderful sister, job, Jewish mother, or why he broke up with his boyfriend, I always found you were wasting your time.

The last thing in the matching ritual that I discovered was that if you don't have sex on the first or second date, you never will. You may become friends- good, even best friends; but without actually 'doing it,' you never will have sex with that person. Men are not all like catholic virgins who believe in a prolonged dating romance sans sex.

Another thing I learned quickly was that if after sex, the person says something to the effect of: "Hey, that was good. We should get together again some time. Give me your telephone number." That 'some time' will probably be 'never,' and the call will never come.

I guess that in straight bars the search for Mr. or Miss 'Right' is pretty much the same. Guys are looking for the girl of their dreams, and the girls are searching for that special person. Straights may have it a bit easier, however, because in their life-times they may not have to go cruising as frequently. Without marriage or the formal acknowledgment of a partnered relationship, which has the effect of holding couples together, gay men may get caught in the cruising game almost every day of their adult lives. Many gay men in the 1960's were changing relationships as often as they changed pants.

Both guys and gals should beware of the 'Trevor Hilton types' they may run into. My affair with Trevor began on a very cold Saturday night in February at, of course, La Bar. Eleven-thirty p.m. to 12:30 a.m.is usually considered the witching hour on Friday and Saturday nights because that's when the cruising usually slowed down and the serious sex activities began. No one wanted to go home alone after chalking up a big bar tab. Hell, I've seen some good-looking men go home with absolute dogs at 'last call' rather than leaving a bar to stagger home by themselves. Perhaps late at night and when your sufficiently boozed, that dog may appear as a cute golden retriever. It's the next morning when you discover that cute, little puppy you brought home is really a growling Rottweiler.

The witching hour had not started when I first spotted Trevor. He came in through the front door and just stood off to the side by himself. Why none of the two hundred or so guys in the bar didn't immediately seduce him was a mystery to me. No question about it, a good-looking… no, gorgeous… guy like that being alone was unheard of. Was I the only guy who realized that? Truth be told: I couldn't get my eyes off him. He was that one number with a capital 'N' that stood out.

His great looks and thick, curly blonde hair flowing out of his beige plaid, flannel cap resembling something Sherlock Holmes might wear added to his unique appearance. He wore a coat, the style of which I had not seen anyone but the Beetles wear before. It looked like a pea coat, but the brown plaid coat had buttons to his chin and a scarf was wrapped around where a collar would be. The coat probably was too tight on him, thus making him appear to be a mummy wrapped up for arctic weather.

My glances in his direction quickly turned to staring. He must have realized it also because our eyes quickly locked. He smiled. I turned away embarrassed. He walked through the crowd and wiggled his way to stand between my chair and the next.

"Hello."

"Ah, Hi."

"You interested?"

"Ah, interested," I stammered. "In what?"

"In leaving this stifling bar with me this minute or making me take off my coat and staying here with you as long as it takes."

"As long as what takes?"

He smiled. "As long as it takes for me to convince you to go someplace else with me." I noticed that he had a distinct accent, but I could not identify it.

I smiled at him. "I'm sorry but I don't know you."

"True. I'm Trevor Hilton. And you are?"

"I'm Cee Jay Seton," I said extending my hand.

"Good. Now that we know one another, do you want to leave with me, Cee Jay Seton?"

"If I said 'no,' would you ask someone else here to go with you?"

"No."

"Why not?"

"Because I'm not interested in anyone else here, Cee Jay Seton."

I swallowed the last of my drink and began sucking on the lemon peel. "Okay, what the hell. Let's blow this joint."

He smiled. I snickered back and we went from the overly hot, smoke filled, crowded bar out to the cold, quiet street. We seemed to be walking aimlessly and in silence for a few minutes.

"Thanks for leaving with me," Trevor said. "Are you in the mood for a big cup of hot tea? I am, but I don't know this part of the city. Do you?"

"mmm. Hot tea after two martinis does sound good, but I don't know of any tea houses in the neighborhood. If you don't mind climbing to a fourth- floor tenement apartment, I can make us some nice chamomile in my place. I live in the next block."

"That really sounds more interesting than going to my third-floor walk-up furnished studio on West Fortieth."

On the way to my place, I learned that Trevor was from Australia and had moved to New York only two weeks ago. He told me that he was an operating room nurse at St. Vincent's Hospital. He explained that he graduated from a university in Melbourne with a degree in nursing and became a registered nurse and took studies for a Master's degree in Canberra. "I'm not sure if my wardrobe, which I bought in England, is quite appropriate in New York," he added.

"I was wondering about that," I said with a smile.

When we entered my apartment, he immediately took his coat, hat and scarf off and tossed them on the futon. I noticed that he wore tight fitting jeans and an apricot colored shirt with snap buttons and a round top with no collar. All his clothes seemed tight which emphasized a well-built structure that I was itching to touch all over.

He followed me into the kitchen where I put a pan of water on the stove for our tea. We sat at the kitchen table while the water boiled and the tea bags seeped. I suggested that we take our cups into the living room, but Trevor said that he was happy to stay in the kitchen and talk. And talk we did for over an hour.

He told me that he had lived in London for six months before flying to New York. He explained that as a male, operating room nurse he could quickly get employment any where in the world and that it was his goal to see and experience as much of the world as he possibly could. I remember thinking at the time that perhaps he was not the type to settle down in any kind of relationship, but I was so fascinated with him that I quickly let that thought go.

I told him about my background and what I was doing at the University. I told him that while I was really enjoying life in the Village, I probably would move to some small college and town after earning my degree.

Eventually, we began to hold hands. He then leaned across the table. Instinctively, I also moved in closer to him. We were locked in one another's eyes before he kissed me. We both stood and fully embraced. We kissed warmly and lovingly and we began to run our hands over one another's body.

I lead him to the bedroom. The sex we had was filled with passion. Trevor was a wonderful lover. We seemed very compatible. When we finished our love making, I asked him to spent the night rather than going out into the cold. He quickly accepted my offer, and we fell asleep happy and contented in one another's arms.

When I awoke the next morning, my first thought was of my new bedmate. I wanted to cuddle with him again, to see and feel his warm body next to mine. Rolling over and feeling under the covers; however, I realized he was not there. I leaned over the bed to see if any of his clothes were still on the floor where he left them after quickly disrobing last night. The floor was empty.

Oh, my god! I thought. *Did he get up and leave while I was asleep? Why? When? Perhaps he robbed me. Was I a fool for inviting a practical stranger to stay the night? But if he were going to steal anything from me, what could he possibly have taken? The only item I have of any value is my electric typewriter.*

I jumped out of the bed and quickly put on my underwear and shirt.

"Good morning, Cee Jay." His voice was coming from the living room, but I could not see him.

He was laying on his back flat on the floor, fully clothed.

"Trevor. I didn't hear you getting out of bed. What are you doing on the floor?

"Well, my dear, I didn't want to disturb your sleep, so I grabbed my duds, got dressed in here and am now doing my usual morning exercises. Do you care to join me on this cold floor?"

"Ah, no thank you. How long have you been in here?"

"Oh, only a half hour or so." He raised his arm to grab my hand. "Did you miss me, love?"

"Actually, I had evil thoughts of you deserting me in the middle of the night."

"After last night, I don't think I would ever desert you."

"You're very sweet," I said as I attempted to pull him up. It didn't take much effort, and as soon as he was standing, he embrace me tenderly and we kissed on the lips. He then slapped me on my ass.

"Now get some clothes on so we can either go out for breakfast or we can cook in together."

"What time it, anyway?" I asked.

He walked back into the bedroom to get his watch which was still on the night stand. *How could I have thought this great guy would steal anything from me and leave?* I thought.

"According to my Mickey Mouse watch, it is 9:30." Trevor said.

"I seldom sleep this late, I bet it was the tea."

"Or the nice time we had in bed. I bet that's it. We both slept soundly because we were happy and content."

"I usually go down stairs to my friend Paul's apartment for Sunday brunch. Since his lover died less than a year ago, Paul and I have more or less started a routine of having Sunday brunch together. I'm sure he wouldn't mind if you joined us and I would like you to meet him. He's still going through a bad period of adjustment, and you would be more than a welcome diversion."

"Well, I am open to the invitation."

"Good, I'll give him a call now and tell him to set a third place at the table.

Paul's Italian and a great cook."

Paul was delighted to hear that I had met someone and glad that Trevor would be joining us for our regular Sunday brunch and get-together. "Yes, we'll be down at 10:30. Trevor says he's starving. Bye."

As soon as I put the phone down, Trevor grabbed me. "Don't get dressed just now. I want to make love to you again before breakfast."

"You do, do you," I said smiling as he smothered me with a kiss.

The unusual aspect of our passion was that he practically ripped my jockeys off, while he remained fully dressed except for the fact that I was able to undo his buckle and lower his jeans and shorts to his calves. Other than the fact that we both reached orgasm quickly, our love making was filled with passion and emotion. It was mutually exciting, compatible, and wonderful.

Afterward, I washed my face and got dressed quickly. We knocked on 3-A at 10:40.

Paul and Trevor seemed to quickly become friends. Paul was fascinated to learn that Trevor was Australian and wanted to know all about Sydney and Ares Rock. Trevor loved talking about the didgeridoo and the aborigines.

As usual, Paul made a pitcher of mimosas. In the kitchen we sat down to one of Paul's great ham, cheese, and red pepper omelets, which were served with Italian sausages and fresh baked rolls.

"I bet you guys met at La Bar last night," Paul said while pouring our coffee.

"Well, we did say 'Hello' there but immediately left to ah… go… ah, elsewhere," I stammered.

"Say no more. I understand. And believe me, I probably would have done the same thing if I were in your position." Paul turned to Trevor. "I known how Cee Jay found La Bar, but what about you, Trevor? How did you happen to stumble into our little, gay tavern on the corner last night?"

"Easy. I never travel without my **Damron Guide**. I used it in Canberra when I first came out, used it in London for the six months I lived there, and yesterday used it to begin exploring what the famous Greenwich Village has to offer."

"Ah, yes. **Damron Guide**, the gay man's source of new and wonderful places to go."

"What is this guide you're talking about?"

"Trevor, you'll have to excuse Mary, here. She's an innocent virgin, you know," Paul said.

Trevor explained. "It's a book that lists gay bars, hotels, restaurants, bath houses, etc. in cities around the world. They publish books just for certain countries and in some cases even for specific cities that have large gay populations. Almost every community has at least one gay bar. In New York City there must be at least one hundred bars. **Damron** is indispensable for the gay traveler like myself. One of the problems with it, however, is that gay bars come and go rather quickly. You may be looking for a certain place that someone recommended to you and when you get the address listed in **Damron** find out that it closed a few months ago or was turned into a church."

"And in the case of New York, the church was changed into a very popular gay disco," Paul said.

"Cee Jay, I need to use your phone to check with my answering service to see if I'm needed this afternoon at Saint Vincent's. I'm on call today." He got up from the table. "Paul, it has been a pleasure meeting you. I hope the three of us can get together again for one of your great breakfasts or just do something else together."

Back upstairs, Trevor made the call and found out that he was needed in the hospital at four o'clock to assist in a transplant operation. Before he left, however, we had sex one more time. This time, it lasted longer, and was better than our morning session, but it left me exhausted. I wondered how Trevor was able to go to work and perform at the level of perfection his work demanded. Before he left, we did exchange telephone numbers and the usual promises of calling one another; but with Trevor I knew he was sincere and would indeed call me. And if he didn't, I would call him because I knew that I really liked him and loved being in his company.

I was thrilled to hear his Australian accent Wednesday afternoon. He telephoned to asked if he could visit that evening, and, of course, I said 'yes.'

He was in my apartment just a few minutes before we were naked and cuddling in bed. Throughout our love making, he kept telling me how much he liked me, how much he had missed me between Sunday afternoon and now, how he enjoyed having sex with me, and how compatible we seemed. Naturally I agreed with him on all points.

When we finished in the bedroom, we went into the living room. He was pleased to learn that we also shared a taste for classical and show music. I made tea, lit two votive candles, and we spent a pleasant, romantic evening just listening to records. He said that he would purchase a few albums at the record store next time he came to my place.

He called again on Friday, to say that he was not working on Saturday and asked if he could see me Saturday and stay over- night. I really wanted to see him, but I had a lot of reading to do and one paper to write and probably would not be good company.

"I understand how difficult and important your studies are, and I promise I will not be bothersome…. Well, maybe just a little when I arrive; but I'll bring a book to curl up with while you slave away at your studies. Later, I'll treat you to a dinner at a great Italian restaurant I heard about last night."

"Honestly, Trevor. I don't know if I can work with you in the apartment."

"That's just the point: you don't know. Neither do I know how it would work out, but why don't we give it a… 'a trial' and see how it works out. If it works for both of us, great; if not, we won't get together in the future when you have school work that has to be done."

I paused to contemplate all he said and all he was implying. "What's the name of the restaurant you're going to treat me at?"

"Momma Leone's."

"I've heard of it. Okay, you can come over for 'a trial' visit."

"Super! I'll bring a toothbrush and razor. I'll see you around noon on Saturday."

Before hanging up, I said, "Trevor, I really do want to see you."

I stayed at the Library late on Friday doing the necessary research I needed. I started writing the paper as soon as I got up on Saturday. By 11:30 I was ready for a break. I had a light brunch, shaved, showered, and dressed for my date with Trevor. I knew he would want to have sex- as I wanted to also- as soon as he arrived. After that would come 'the trial': Could I work while he read or just kept away from me? Could I stay away from him?

My buzzer sounded at exactly one o'clock. By five after we were kissing and groping, by ten after we were striping our clothes off, and by fifteen after one we were involved in wild, wicked, but wonderful sex.

Penetrating Trevor was the ultimate sexual experience for me. I felt so completely attached to him as with no one else I had ever been with before. Holding him in my arms, running my fingers through his curly blonde hair, kissing his warm lips, sucking on his beautifully engorged and shaped penis were amazing experiences which all seemed greater each time we made love. In a strange sense, I felt that I possessed him; that he was mine; someone that I could protect and cherish.

When we were ready for orgasm, we both ejaculated simultaneously. We lay side by side holding hands and marveling at the wonderful experience we had shared. I think that I may have said "Wow!" a few times.

After a while Trevor got up and went to the bathroom to wash. He returned with a wash clothe and hand towel and proceeded to wipe cum from my navel area, hands and penis. When he finished, he grabbed me by the hand and pulled me off the bed. "Okay. It's time for us to get dressed, and for you to get to your school work."

'The trial' worked extremely well. I was able to concentrate on my readings and papers while at the kitchen table, while Trevor remained at the other end of the apartment reading the newspaper and book which he brought with him. After about four hours I was ready for a break and went into the living room to tell him that I was through working for the day. I found him sound asleep in the recliner. He looked so cute, I felt guilty in waking him.

"Hey, Sleepy. Wake up." I gently shook his shoulder.

He opened his sapphire eyes and smiled. "What time is it?"

"It's time for you to take me to Momma Leone's."

At the restaurant Trevor asked me if I ever had skied. I told him that I was a pretty good water skier but also enjoyed snow skiing even though I had only snow skied a few times in my life.

"Great, because I have never been on skis, but that is something I want to do while I'm in this part of the United States. Why don't you and I go skiing next weekend?"

"Hey, that sounds like fun, but I don't know if I can get away for a full weekend. And I don't know where we could go, and even if we could, neither of us has a car, so how would we get there? Remember, I'm a poor student, I'm not sure I could financially swing it."

"I've figured all that out. There's a new ski resort in northern New Jersey. It is a Playboy Club. They have a hotel, pool, restaurant, and even a mountain for skiing. I'll pay for a rental car as well as the hotel. All you would have to pay for is a few meals and whatever. Fifty dollars, at most."

"That sounds very tempting, Trevor. I would love a break from New York, and the thought of being with you in a hotel for two nights is grand." I paused. "I'll certainly think about it and check on my NYU duties. Can I give you a definite answer on Wednesday?"

"Definitely!"

"By the way, what did you mean a moment ago when you said 'while I'm in this part of the United States'?"

"Well, unless I'm mistaken, they don't have ski slopes in Los Angeles or Miami. I'll be going to those cities when I leave Saint Vincent's. As I told you when we met, my goal is to travel around the world and see and experience as much as possible."

"Yeah, I do remember you telling me that, but I guess I had put it out of mind. How long do you plan on staying in the New York area?"

"Maybe six months or so. It really depends on how things go here."

"Oh, I was....." I didn't finish my sentence.

It seemed as though Trevor was reading my mind. "You will be getting your doctorate in less than a year, Cee Jay. Will you be staying in New York?"

"No. I'll probably get a college position in some small town far from here."

Trevor grabbed my hand and held it firmly. "There you go, Mate. So let's make the most of our time together." He paused and then added, "Okay?"

We did go to the Playboy Resort in Sussex County, New Jersey, the following Friday for two glorious nights; however, it was too warm for making snow and it rained on Saturday. What snow there was turned into slush and mud. We stayed in bed making love most of the weekend, but we did have some excellent meals and thoroughly enjoyed the heated swimming pool, sauna, fitness center, and the cocktail lounge.

Trevor dropped me off in the Village around five o'clock and said that he had to return the rented car before six. I really felt disappointed and depressed that he had to leave. I wanted him to stay with me forever. The thought of his leaving New York in a few months was difficult to accept. I was lonely and had to talk to someone, so I called Paul and invited him up for a cocktail or two or three.

Paul said that he was anxious to hear about my 'get away weekend' and had something to tell me also.

I knew that Paul had been depressed since George's death. He no longer went to La Bar or any of the other bars in town. He confided in me sufficiently for me to know that he had no interest in meeting other men. I also knew that he had been to a psychologist and attended group grieving sessions. When I opened the door that Sunday evening, his eyes were bloodshot, and it was apparent that he had been crying for some time.

"I'm moving back to Wisconsin as soon as school's out."

How could I talk about my joy of having – but soon to lose- a new boyfriend when Paul had been going through so much. His decision to leave his teaching position and the City were far greater than my immediate concerns.

"The apartment just has too many memories for me," he began crying again. "I sometimes wake up in the middle of the night and reach over to touch him, but he's not there."

Paul explained that his brother had been encouraging him to return to Madison since the accident, but he liked his school, the Village neighborhood, and all his friends too much to leave.

Sal had convinced him to move back to Madison where they could share an apartment, and Paul could get away from everything that reminded him of George and the life they had and the plans they had of a future together. It was time for Paul to start a new life.

I knew that I would miss Paul tremendously. I also knew that I had to accept the fact that any long-term relationship with Trevor also was not going to happen.

I did continue to occasionally date Trevor, but our dates became more social than physical. I became more concerned with working on my dissertation than on seeing him. I guess our real breakup began when he told me one Sunday afternoon that he had begun to date someone else, an intern at the hospital. "I hope you're okay with that, Cee Jay," he nonchalantly stated.

But I was not 'okay' with it. I tried to act as though it were, but I was hurt deeply. I definitely could not have sex with him again now that I knew he was doing it with another person. The mere fact that he so openly admitted it to me was an indication to me that he thought of our relationship as less than I did.

Coincidentally, Trevor said his final 'goodbyes' to me on Wednesday, and Diane and I drove Paul to JFK for his flight to Madison on Friday morning. The three of us were tearful while waiting in the terminal. Paul promised to keep in touch, as we did also.

Paul and I stayed in touch, mostly through Christmas cards with newsletters for a few years. He seemed happy to be living in Madison. The last card I got from him announced that he had become the principal of a suburban junior high and was in a new relationship with a young pediatrician. "We are planning to buy a house together in Madison," he wrote. The PS at the end of the letter read: "My brother Sal sends his love. He and the girl he has been living with for over a year are getting married in February."

I never heard from Trevor after he moved on to South Beach, Florida.

Chapter Twelve

FAST FORWARD TO JAMIE AGAIN

After that day in Asbury Park, I seldom saw Jamie. When we did talk, it was only superficial and brief. As my assistant teaching duties increased and I devoted more time to my dissertation, I went to the bar less. Once, when I inquired about Jamie, I was told that he hadn't been around in a while. One of his hustler friends told me that he heard that Jamie was going to a new piano bar uptown now. So it was that I never saw Jamie or heard about him in many months.

When I received my degree, I got a position teaching at a small college in Pennsylvania, and Jamie Roberts as well as my Greenwich Village apartment, and all the guys I had met at La Bar became a pleasant memory.

Several years later I accepted a position as department chairman and teacher in a high school in northern new Jersey. I taught four classes, one of which was senior Advanced English. I was anxious to return to the challenges of the high school classroom.

The day before school started, I checked the class rosters to familiarize myself with student names in an effort to more quickly get to know them. One name immediately caught my attention. The name "Barbara Roberts' appeared on the Advanced Placement class list. An image of Jamie Roberts quickly came into mind. Jamie, the skinny kid with acne who told me he was bisexual on the beach in Asbury Park. I toyed with the idea that that this girl was the one who Jamie had on his lap as a baby in the picture he had shown me. I remember that the girl's name was Barbara. Jamie had said, "We named her after Melissa's mother." *No,* I thought, *this couldn't be the same Barbara Roberts. Both names are common; it's just a strange coincidence; but enough years have passed so that the beautiful little girl in the picture probably would now be around high school age. Strange, but interesting to think about.*

The next day, as I called attendance and studied each face carefully in order to connect a face with each name, I was startled to see a beautiful young lady who responded to the name 'Barbara Roberts.'

"Please call me Barbie, if you don't mind, Dr. Seton," she said. I recalled that Jamie had called the baby in photo his 'Barbie doll.'

After a few weeks, I was extremely pleased with my Advanced Placement class, particularly a student named Barbara or 'Barbie.' I learned that everyone called her that. Barbie was quick to enter a discussion on everything from witches of Salem to the Transcendentalists in Concord. Her writing demonstrated a flair for the creative. I learned that she was a popular cheerleader, a good basketball player, and a member of the student council. When I asked for volunteers to start up an after-school peer-tutoring group for freshmen who needed help in writing, Barbie was the first to volunteer. When she said that she would be glad to help out, one other girl and two boys also volunteered. Her leadership skills were obvious.

In early October, the school had a "Back to School Night" for parents and their children. The students were to attend all of their scheduled classes with one or both of their parents. Each teacher was to prepare a short lesson that highlighted his or her class in fifteen minutes. I was anxious to discover who Barbie's parents were and if they would show up in my classroom with their bright daughter. I was disappointed, however, when they did not attend my 15-minute 'get-to-know-you' sample class.

"Back to School Night" ended with a brief reception in the cafeteria. I was just about to leave when I saw Barbie with two grown-ups holding her hands on either side approach me. "I am so sorry we missed your class, Dr. Seton," Barbie said as they came near. "My parents had to see one of my brother's teachers during your period three."

"Cee Jay!" the man with her yelled loud enough for everyone in the cafeteria to hear. He embraced me with a bear hug. "If Barbie had told me the names of her teachers, I would have been here to see you long ago. Man, isn't this coincidental! My 'Jorsy' friend turns out to be my little girl's teacher, and we all live in 'Jorsy.'" I could tell that he was deliberately emphasizing 'Jorsy' for "New Jersey,' the way he did at La Bar. "How's this for coincidence, huh? Melissa, honey, this Cee Jay, the man I used to tell you about when we lived in New York." Melissa extended a warm handshake.

"What's going on here? Am I in an alternate universe?" Barbie was confused, amazed, and amused.

"Sweetheart, your teacher here, Cee jay Seton is your daddy's long- lost pal from the days when we lived in New York. We used to… a… we used to hang out together in Manhattan. Isn't that right, Cee Jay?"

"Yes, I guess you can say that." I gave Melissa a quick glance. The expression on her face told me all I needed to know. Everything about Jamie's life that I remembered was true. He had not fabricated the story of his being married and having a child. "Did I hear correctly? You have a son attending this school also?"

"Yes," Melissa said, "our son Robbie is a junior now. He is a good student, but seems to be having some problems in his third period trigonometry class, so we went there rather than your English class. But if we had known that you were Barbie's teacher, we definitely would have been there." She paused. "So how is Barbie doing in your class, Cee Jay? May I call you Cee Jay?"

"Of course, you may. Please. In a word Barbie is an excellent student. One of the best. She must take after you, Melissa, not this big, klutzy husband of yours. Right, Jamie?" I said as I gave him a loving punch on his arm.

"Hey, watch it, doc. Your talking to a parent who now has an associate's degree, and Melissa is working toward an MBA at Montclair State," Jamie said proudly.

"Wow! That's great. Who would have known? I'm very happy for both of you."

Just then a tall, skinny youngster with a bit of acne approached us. "And here's the youngest member of the Roberts clan." Jamie introduced me to his son who enthusiastically shook my hand.

Robert Roberts looked exactly as his father must have looked at his age. I stepped back a little so that I could fully grasp the connections between what I remembered about Jamie, and now his daughter, son, and wife. I realized the years were good to Jamie. He seemed to have a happy aura. He was still youthful looking. Gone were his facial blemishes. Gone was the stringy, dyed blonde hair down to his shoulders. Now his hair was a natural light brown with just a few streaks of gray starting to show around the temples. It was thick but perfectly trimmed. He had put on enough pounds to pass as a man who spent some time in a gym. He wore tight-fitting jeans, a long-sleeve white shirt, and a blue striped tie. He seemed to blend in with the other dads in this conservative, upper-middle class suburban community.

I was still processing all of this when the principal made the PA announcement thanking the parents and children for attending the Back to School event and saying that the cafeteria was closing in five minutes. Most of the students and their parents had left any way. We were among the few stragglers left in the lunch room. As we started out of the building, Jamie reached into his wallet and gave me his business card. "Please call me, Cee Jay. We'll have to have you over for dinner sometime soon. We have a lot of catching up to do." He paused. "And thanks for being Barbie's teacher. She often mentions how she enjoys her English class but never mentioned your name."

As we parted in the parking lot, Jamie said, "Gee, Cee Jay, it's really been great seeing you again. Be sure to call me soon. You have my number."

The truth of the matter is that I had no intention of calling Jamie. When I got home, I pulled his card from my pants pocket where I put it without looking at it at the school. It read: "Roberts Real Estate Development and Construction, LLC."

I had seen Jamie and I saw his family, but I could not quite accept the transformation from the Jamie I knew in Greenwich Village and Asbury Park to the man I met at the high school. How did this incredible transformation take place? After school the next day, I drove to the address on Jamie's business card. It was on the outskirts of town, but I readily found it; it was real. A large sign announced to anyone passing on the highway that Jamie Roberts was real. The building was larger than I expected; it appeared to be half office and half warehouse. Three pick-up trucks bearing the company name were parked on the side.

A few days later my curiosity was still keen, so after checking Barbie's records in the school office, I learned where she lived. Early that evening I drove passed the house. It was a red brick colonial. A basketball backboard and hoop hung in the center of a two-car garage. The spacious lawn was perfectly manicured as wee the shrubs and flower beds. The most striking feature of the property for me was the neat, white picket fence surrounding three sides of the house. I remembered that Jamie told me of his wish of having a white picket fence around a home in the suburbs where he and the person he loved would raise a family.

I did not call Jamie. I thought that I would find it very awkward going to his house. It was awkward enough having his beautiful and very intelligent daughter in my class every day. On a few occasions, I ran into Robbie in the halls. I learned that Robbie was on the basketball team. Robbie always gave me a big smile and greeting. "Hello, Dr. Seton, you're looking sharp today" he would say, or "Nice suit, Dr. S."

One day Robbie caught me in the lunch room. "Hey, Dr. Seton. My dad wants to know when you're coming to our place to shoot some hoops with us." I just smiled and said that it would be sometime soon. I really thought that it would be never. *Yes,* I thought, *Robbie has his dad's personality; Barbara has Melissa's brains and wisdom. Jamie had said that Melissa was working on a MBA. I wondered what kind of work she was doing now. Surely, an MBA candidate does not do typing in her brick colonial house. Maybe she runs the business end of Roberts Real Estate Development and Construction, LLC.*

My telephone rang at ten o'clock at night the day after Robbie asked when I was going to visit them to play basketball. "Hey, Cee Jay, It's me, Jamie. You remember me, the skinny hustler from the Village. The kid you wouldn't have sex with even though I didn't want any money from you." His words were bold and slurred. From the background noise I heard, I assumed he was calling from a tavern.

"Of course, I remember you, Jamie. How are you besides being drunk?"

"Hey, I'm not drunk! Not yet, at any rate. But that's no way to talk to an old friend you haven't seen in years. Accusing him of being drunk! You sound like my wife." There was a long pause during which neither of us knew what to say. "Hello, you still there, Cee Jay?"

"Yes. I'm still here, Jamie. I'm sorry I accused you of being drunk."

"Well, maybe I am… a little," Jamie admitted. "You know what I'm drinking? A martini! That was always your pissy- ass drink. Do you still drink martinis, Cee Jay? I drink martinis now, Cee Jay. And you know what: every time I drink a martini, I think of you. Tonight, I've already had two in order to get up enough nerve to call you." There was a long pause. I had a vision of Jamie trying to stand up at the pay phone. "I want to see, you, man."

"I would like to see you too, Jamie. Really, I would, but not at your house. Not having dinner with your wife and kids. Not playing hoops with you and Robbie. It's just too damn awkward for me that way."

"Right. I hear you. It probably would be damn awkward for me too. So, how can we get together?"

"Well, how about you leave the bar you're in and going home safely right now. Have a good night's sleep. Since you got my number from a telephone book, you know where I live. Can you come to my place tomorrow evening?"

"Can I come over to your house now?

"Absolutely not! It's too late." I paused. "And I think I'd prefer you perfectly sober. Come tomorrow at 7:30. And, Jamie… I'd really like to see you again."

"Okay. It's a date. I'll see you at 7:30. I promise that you will not detect a hint of booze on me."

After I hung up, I wondered if I had done the right thing. It was clear that he wanted to see me again. I wanted to see him. I didn't know what would happen, what we'd talk about, whether it was wise, whether he would tell Melissa. I knew that I was attracted to him at the 'Back to School Night.' At school the next day I was nervous and anxious. I had a feeling that I had not experienced in years. I worried that he might not show up at my house that night.

Just as he had been prompt in showing up for our date to go to Asbury Park, my doorbell rang at exactly 7:30. Jamie seemed even better looking than when I saw him at school. He had a slight five o'clock shadow which gave him a more rugged appearance. Rather than wearing tight jeans, he wore beige Dockers and a light green sport shirt. Rather than sneakers, he had a pair of brown loafers. Rather than a hint of gin, I detected a hint of Brut.

I ushered him into the living room and to a sofa opposite the fireplace in which I had lit some logs while waiting for him. I sat on the sofa close to him. I extended my arm on the sofa back but did not touch him.

We talked at length. He told me about Father O'Hearn, his pastor, who liked his work at the church in Brooklyn. Jamie told me that the reason he didn't go to the La Bar was that he started working full-time at the church and its elementary school. He was naturally skilled with plumbing, painting, fixing minor electrical problems, and the heating and air conditioning systems in the church, rectory and school. Jamie told me that when he told the priest that his wife was pregnant with their second child, Father O'Hearn motivated him to think more seriously about going to a community college to study construction trades. The priest helped him with the application and even gave him a Christmas bonus big enough to pay for a semester.

"Never did Father O'Hearn ask me about my religion; but when Robbie was born, he asked me if I wanted him to baptize Robbie as he had Barbara. I felt honored that he would do all of this for me and Melissa. After Robert Roberts was baptized... hey, how do you like the name? I thought it was cool!... Father O'Hearn started helping Melissa also. He saw to it that the two kids got day care at the school while Melissa started courses in business part-time. Father O'Hearn loved our kids and delighted in seeing them play in his rectory. I lost a good friend when Father O'Hearn died. He was a good man, Cee Jay. A real man of God. Shortly after he died, we moved to New Jersey and the rest, as they say, is history."

I asked him if he ever went back to La Bar or saw any of his friends from there. I wanted to know if he remained a male prostitute after we lost touch. "No, I stopped going to all the bars after a while. After Robbie was born, I just became too busy working at the church and going to school at night. I did on occasion stop in for a 'quicky' in some tea room here and there, but gave that up too. It seemed dirty and degrading to me. And then, when the whole AIDS thing started, I just thought it was too dangerous, so I became an at-home dad and husband. Melissa was all I needed and on days when that didn't work for her, my hand got a workout on my dick. Funny thing, though, I couldn't jerk off without thinking about men."

At this point I felt the need for a drink and offered to make a martini for him also. I was surprised when he said that he would be fine with just a Pepsi or Coke, if I had it. I said that I did and excused myself to go into the kitchen. As I was leaving, he said, "I think I had too much gin last night." I smiled knowingly.

When I returned with my martini and his soda, I offered a toast. "Here's to you and me." I paused. "And to the guys we knew at La Bar." Our glasses touched.

"And God. Let's not forget God in this equation," Jamie added. "The big guy upstairs has been very good to me."

My arm dropped from the back of the sofa to his neck and with my hand I pushed him closer to me. For a long moment we just looked into one another's eyes before our lips met. We kissed long and passionately before I began to unbutton his shirt. He obliged by removing it entirely. I stared at his rippled chest before lightly kissing and then squeezing his nipples with my teeth. He pulled me to his mouth and we began kissing again. Kissing Jamie felt so good, so natural, I got lost in the thought of devouring him. He reached for my crotch and was pleased that I was already erect. We continued to kiss as he tried to undo my belt and zipper. When he managed to grab my swollen penis in his hand, I suggested that we go upstairs to my bedroom. He was standing in an instant and disrobing as we practically ran upstairs.

He had his shoes and socks off but kept his white Jockey briefs on. I undressed more slowly gazing intently at his perfectly sculptured body. "What?" he said embarrassingly.

"You have a beautiful body. How did you get from the flat-chested skinny kid I saw on the beach one day to having this great body?" I put both arms around his chest and back.

"I guess I just grew up." Jamie kissed me again. "Construction work is not easy, but it builds muscles. I also go to the gym a few times a week."

I practically threw him on my bed. After a lingering kiss, my lips moved to his ear lobes, then to the side of his face. I licked at his five o'clock shadow. My lips moved to his smooth, almost hairless chest. I played with his nipples, kissing and lightly biting them. I licked at his navel as I slightly lift the front of his briefs. My mouth slid the outline of his cock. With my teeth I grabbed his shorts and slowly released his throbbing member. Immediately, my lips were around the head of his beautiful dick and I sucked longingly. He was moaning softly, letting me know that he was enjoying this as much as I was.

After a short time, Jamie pulled back. "Not yet!" he exclaimed. "I don't want to come this soon." He indicated that I should lay next to him. We kissed again and then he began to go down on me. His warm mouth captured my cock. It felt heavenly. We repositioned our bodies so that we could suck on one another. I took his balls into my mouth and licked on one, then the other, then both together.

"Yes, Oh, yes!" Jamie moaned. "That's what I like." We stayed locked in the '69' position for several minutes before Jamie broke loose again. "Man, you are so hot; but I want this to continue. Let's not come right now. Okay, Cee Jay?" He sat up on the bed.

I put my arms around him; he turned and then put his knees on either side of me. I pulled him up closer to me so that I could get his cock into my mouth once more. With my arms free I played with his chest with one hand and played with his ass with the other. He reached behind to grab my hard manhood. After a while he pulled his dick out of my mouth and slid back a few inches. He seemed too embarrassed to speak but turned his head to the left and right.

"You want something?" I asked.

"I want you to fuck me," he said quietly. "In which table do you keep your stuff?"

"Left one. Top drawer."

He immediately leaned over and retrieved the condoms and lubricant which I always kept handy.

"You have no idea how much I want you to fuck me," Jamie said. "I want to feel you deep inside me. I want us to finally be fully connected."

He had some difficulty rolling the sheath onto my cock. He added some KY to it and then put enough on his fingers to insert into his hole before grabbing my dick and holding it in place as he slowly permitted my cock to enter him. He didn't relax until I was fully in. His expression of determination as he struggled to accept me turned to an expression of joy as he slowly moved his body up and down, feeling my cock inside him fully now.

His own cock, which seemed longer but had less girth than my own, danced in front of me. I grabbed at it to his delight. My other hand moved over his chest. He leaned into me; I enveloped his hot breath.

"This is the way it should be," Jamie whispered in my ear.

"Yes." Was my only response.

Sensing that I wanted to kiss him, he leaned farther to me and in so doing, my cock slid from his butt cheeks. As our lips met, our tongues intertwined. "I love making love with you, Cee Jay," he whispered. "Please fuck me some more," he pleaded.

Jamie turned over on his stomach and raised his backside by getting on his knees. I quickly got behind him on my knees. He was in a perfect position for me to penetrate him again. I found the tube of jelly and put a generous amount on my fingers so that I could spread it around his anus. Before inserting my penis, I played with his cock and balls. I entered him slowly, enjoying every second, every inch. As I slowly got more into him, I felt that I could no longer control my emotions. We were both moaning and panting. Feeling at last his warm semen filling my hand, I pounded on his backside and felt rapturous as I knew I was filling the condom. He turned over on his back as I fell beside him. Neither of us spoke. We lay side by side breathing heavily,

When we turned to look at one another, we were both smiling. "That was incredible!"

"Now you know what we were both missing during those fifteen years," Jamie responded.

I kissed him again. "We'll have to make up for lost time."

"Yes, but let's shower first. I don't want my Jorsy lover to think I stink like a sweaty pig from Secaucus."

It was at that moment, realizing that he had never forgotten that little story I told him so many years ago on the bus going to Asbury Park, that I knew I loved Jamie Roberts. Yes, I loved the sex we just had, but now it was more, much more. I truly loved him, the very essence of who he was. And I knew now that he must have loved me for myself even back then. My epiphany was real, and I knew I would love no one more in my life than Jamie Roberts.

After removing the condom, I led him to the bathroom. I turned on the water to make sure the temperature was right before we both stepped into my walk-in shower. Under the shower we started to kiss again. His body felt perfectly joined to mine. I put both arms around him and rubbed up and down his back. I grabbed and squeezed his buttocks. He squeezed my cock which was almost fully erect. We took turns lathering and washing one another. With the water pouring down on us, I got on my knees and began sucking his cock and balls again. It was so erotic I felt that I would come a second time. Jamie must have felt it too, because he turned around; he spread his legs apart as much as possible in the shower. I lathered lots of soap all over his ass. Seeing the suds on his backside and ass was a unique stimulation. I began kissing his butt cheeks and then moved my tongue to rim his anus. He lifted one leg to put his foot on the wall. As my tongue probed, he kept repeating "Oh, god! God! Cee Jay, that's incredible!"

I replaced my tongue with my fingers. "Fuck me again, Cee Jay. Here in the shower bareback. This time I want to feel your cum in my ass. It's okay. I've been checked out. I'm safe."

"So am I," I said.

I had never been this intimate with another human being since Trevor Hilton. Not only were our bodies feeling the joy of togetherness, but our minds, our souls, seemed united as one. For the first time in my life, I felt what it is like to truly love someone. Once again, I came as soon as Jamie began his orgasm.

We washed off some more and when we got out of the shower, Jamie started to dry me with a towel. I reached for the other towel and did the same for him. We didn't speak until we lay down again on the bed.

I looked at the clock on my night stand and broke our silence. "You know it's 11:30 already."

"That's okay. Luckily, it's Friday, and you don't have to go to school in the morning."

"I wish you could spend the entire night with me," I said.

"Maybe someday we can be together over night, but not tonight. Okay? But I'm in no hurry to run off right now without my glass slipper."

"That's good, because I'm still horny for you," I said half-joking. "Remember we have to make up for those fifteen years."

"I hope we can spend time like this more often. And do it for the rest of our lives," Jamie said. "and I'm not just referring to having sex. I want to be with you. I hope we can be very special friends forever."

"I hope so too, Jamie. Somehow I think it was intended by providence that we should get together."

"You know, it used to hurt back then. I know that you didn't like me when I was hustling in the bars. I wasn't your type. Tonight, I think I know what your type is...was... and I can appreciate that. You like men who are seemingly straight... more mature, more settled in life, more intelligent, more professional, more beefy. All the things I was not back in the '60s. Now, I'm actually glad that we never got together before tonight. It hurt back then because I loved you, but then I was the opposite of what you wanted. Ironically, you were all of the things to me that I wanted to be but at the time could not be. Back then it never could have been more than a one-night affair. Now, we are both ready for one another."

He was silent for a minute. "You know, God has been very good to me. I have a great, kind and understanding wife; two kids that I love; a good business; a fine house; and now He has given me you. Yep, I'm the luckiest guy in the world."

After that we just lay in bed holding hands. Once in a while Jamie would take my hand and kiss it. At times we would just touch or embrace one another. Occasionally, we kissed. Eventually our kisses became more passionate and without giving much thought, we found ourselves having sex for the third time that night. I was engrossed in sucking his cock, when he pulled me to him. "You know what I want to do now?" he asked.

"No," I said playfully. "What would you like to do now? Smoke a cigarette? Have a cup of chamomile tea?"

"Nothing like that," Jamie said as he assumed the '69' position. "I want to taste and swallow your cum."

"God, you're a mind reader," I said. "Let's do it."

We sucked and jerked one another. Occasionally one of us would stop so that our partner could hold off until we were both ready. Our simultaneous orgasms sent shivers through both our bodies. My mouth filled with Jamie's hot sperm. I swallowed as fast as I could to get it all, but when I opened my mouth to breath cum fell from my parted lips. I couldn't get enough of Jamie. I smeared his dick with his cum and sucked longingly to get every last drop of him. There was cum still on our faces when we came together and kissed, wiping excess cum off our faces as we did.

Jamie and I continued to see one another frequently. We went to sporting events together at the high school. Even though Robbie was on the basketball team, Jamie showed a preference for attending home football games.

I had a treadmill and exercise machine in my home, but Jamie persuaded he to join his club so that we could encourage one another on physical fitness. It was also an excuse for us to get together. We would go to the health center in separate cars and leave separately to avoid any suspicion and gossip. After our routine workouts, we would go to the pool and then the sauna. It was difficult to keep our hands off one another at the club, specifically, in the sauna.

We got together at my house at least once a week for sex and two Fridays during November he stayed the whole night. The City of Newark had asked him to be a panel member at a land development and preservation conference, so I took a 'personal day' and the two of us went to Newark on the last Thursday of November and stayed for three nights. Jamie assured me that Melissa knew about our rendezvous. While she wasn't happy about it, she seemed to accept it. Their own love life, including sex, had not been affected by my entrance into their lives. The children saw the relationship between me and Jamie as one of strong, platonic friendship. To my knowledge, neither Barbie nor Robbie discussed it with their friends, and neither demonstrated any indication of our connection at school.

Eventually, I started visiting at his house. Robbie, Jamie and I did get to play basketball in his driveway when it wasn't covered in snow or sleet. Once I was invited and did accept an invitation to have Sunday dinner with the family. There was no awkwardness because Melissa, Barbie, and Robbie treated me as a welcome member of their family. However, I was recognized as an honored guest and sat opposite Jamie at the dining room table. I was a bit surprised to realize that saying grace before meals was a regular routine at the Roberts' household. I held hands with Robbie and Barbie as Jamie said a brief prayer in which he thanked God for making it possible for me to join them.

After a wonderful dinner, Melissa suggested that Jamie, Robbie and I play Scrabble in the living room while she and Barbie cleaned up the dishes. "Be careful with my father, Dr. S, your buddy is a very good Scrabble player. Mom says he cheats, so watch him," Barbie said.

"When we're finished in the kitchen, we'll join you men for Robbie's favorite game which happens to be charades. Do you play charades, Cee Jay?" Melissa asked.

"Sure, I love it, but haven't played in a long time."

Jamie was really good at Scrabble. I thought that being an English teacher I would easily defeat both guys. Both Jamie and Robbie proved to be worthy opponents. Robbie seemed to know where to place those high-scoring letters, and Jamie had a knack of putting together letters to form unusual words. I did make a dictionary challenge over one of his words; but I lost; *jigsaw* really is one word, not two as I contended. Eventually, I did win the game, but not by much.

Robbie seemed to be the reigning champion of charades in the Roberts clan, so it was decided that he and I be on opposing sides. Everyone seemed to agree that it should be

Jamie and I against Melissa, Barbie and Robbie. We had a great deal of fun playing the game; everyone seemed to get a charge out of me trying to get Jamie to guess "You Ain't Nothing but a Hound Dog" and Melissa's trying to have her team understand her attempts at "Hard Rain Gonna Fall." I chided Jamie for using this 1961 Bob Dylan classic, which the kids probably never heard.

During our fun together that day, I noticed that Barbie started referring to me as 'Uncle Cee Jay', but Robbie continued calling me 'Dr. S' at home as he had been doing at school.

I was not invited to spend Thanksgiving with them, but Jamie and I did meet at the high school to watch the high school football team play its final game of the season. That year the senior quarterback was Donavon Rice, who also happened to be a student in my Advanced English class. I was proud to see Donavon play so well and to see him lead 'the Mountaineers' to victory.

A few weeks later Melissa invited me to their home for Christmas Day. I was very happy to be invited and quickly accepted. Getting presents for the children was easy. I gave Barbie *The Prophet*, a book by Kahill Gibran. Recently, Robbie had been expressing an interest in becoming a pilot, so I got him an electric, hand-held game called ***Flight Simulator 1983.*** I had no idea what to get Jamie and Melissa. Finally, on Christmas Eve I bought a large poinsettia plant for Melissa and a bottle of Tanqueray for Jamie.

Their house was beautifully decorated for the holidays. A large Frosty, the Snowman blow up was on the front lawn as well as a huge manger that Jamie had obviously made himself. The interesting thing about it, however, was that there were no statues of Mary, Joseph, or any of the other figures one would expect. However, if you got up close and looked into the creche, one could read a sign written in scroll lettering. It said: "Welcome Jesus into your heart where He always should be." I smiled and thought, *Only Jamie Roberts could come up with something as unique as this.*

Robbie opened the door for me. I immediately heard Christmas music and smelled the wonderful pine logs which were roaring in the fireplace. Surprisingly, Robbie gave me a firm hug and cheerful welcome. He helped me with some of the presents I was holding. He put them on the floor by the tree. Several presents had been opened and the wrappings were scattered about. I was still admiring the decorations on the large, natural fir tree when Barbie came into the living room and also hugged me and kissed me on my cheek. "We're so happy you could join us today, Dr. S. My mom and dad will be here in a minute. They're doing something in the kitchen."

She no sooner said this when the host and hostess appeared. Jamie grabbed my hand and as we shook hands, he pulled me into himself. Melissa hugged and kissed me as Barbie had.

Eventually, drinks were served. The kids had egg nog, Melissa had a Manhattan, and Jamie and I had martinis. I noticed that a camera was sitting on the cocktail table in front of the sofa. Seeing me pick up the camera, Robbie said that it had been given to him as a Christmas present from his parents.

"May I take a picture of all of you around the tree?" I asked.

I didn't have to ask twice because led by Melissa, everyone got into position for a nice family photo. After I took the first picture, Melissa said, "Robbie, why don't you put the camera on the tripod and set the shutter on time exposure so you and Cee Jay can all be in a picture with all of us?"

"That's a great idea, Honey. Cee Jay get over here," Jamie said.

I was happy to be in a photo with the whole family, but I deliberately stood next to Melissa. I did not want any picture taken with me standing between Jamie and Melissa. *The implications of such a pose might be misconstrued*, I thought.

"Okay, I'll set the shutter for ten seconds, so when I jump into the picture, smile," Robbie directed.

We did smile and as the flash went off, we all said "cheese" except for Jamie who shouted "sex!" The kids and I laughed at Jamie, but Melissa gave him a dirty look.

Jamie stuck his tongue out and smiled at his wife. "Hey, sex is way better than cheese."

In the dining room, Jamie's prayer which was said while we were still standing was amusing as well as spiritual. In it he again thanked God for his family's blessings and my sharing this day with them, but he also made a few remarks about the gifts that were exchanged. He ended by saying, "And please Jesus, when Cee Jay takes my boy skiing next week may they both come home safely." Robbie, who was holding my hand lightly during the grace, squeezed tightly before saying "Amen." Robbie looked at me and smiled sheepishly as we sat down for our wonderful turkey dinner.

I had almost forgotten the conversation Robbie and I had the previous week about his interest in learning to ski and my telling him how much I liked a ski resort in Pennsylvania. When he asked if I would take him there and teach him how to ski, I said "Sure, we'll have to do that sometime." Robbie, quickly had asked, "What about between Christmas and New Years."

Without giving much thought, I said "Sure" and moved on to something else.

But Robbie had remembered and obviously had even discussed it with his parents. I suddenly felt trapped by my own words. I could not let the boy down.

Our one-day excursion to the Poconos became the topic of major conversation at the table. Jamie gushed how wonderful it was that I was treating son to this adventure. Melissa said that she too was excited about Robbie learning to ski. She said that one of his Christmas presents was a pair of long johns to wear for the trip. Barbie's present was a pair of ski gloves.

Oh, my God. What have I gotten myself into? I thought.

After a wonderful Christmas dinner and lingering conversation, Robbie and Jamie went up to his bedroom to play the flight simulation game I had given Robbie. Barbie excused herself, saying she was tired and wanted to start reading the book I gave her.

Melissa and I decided to clear the dining room, put dishes in the dishwasher, and get rid of some of the wrappings on the living room floor. She shared with me some of her stories of growing up in West Virginia and how she and Jamie moved to New York. She related to me how poor she and Jamie were and how difficult it was when the children were babies. "Only with God's help and the love that Jamie and I had did we survive through the sixties," she said.

"I wish now that I had the opportunity to know Jamie better back then and that you and I could have met."

"It's strange. I know that Jamie met a lot of men back then. He had to. But you, Cee Jay, were the only man he ever talked to me about."

Looking out the living room picture window, we saw that pellets of hail were falling rather rapidly.

"I better hit the road before this storm makes driving impossible. My dog Checkers is probably wondering where I am."

Melissa got my coat from the foyer closet. She helped me put it on. I called my goodbyes upstairs. Robbie went to the top of the stairs to remind me that we were going to the Poconos to ski during the Christmas break. Jamie called down that because business was slow this time of year, he might go along with us. "I'll call you and we can firm up the plans."

At the door, Melissa gave me a kiss on the cheek and softly said, "If I have to share Jamie's love with anyone, Cee Jay, I am glad it is with you."

The End

More fun reading…..

Greenwich Village Tales ends on Christmas Day. Jamie's son, Robbie, is excited to go skiing with Cee Jay. Then Jamie says that he may join them.

What was planned as a one-day trip for Robbie becomes much more than a lesson in how to ski. Author Chuck Walko continues the story of Cee Jay, Jamie, and Robbie in another novel, ***Robbie Keeps the Key***. At first Robbie has to deal with the revelation that his father is bisexual and Cee Jay is his Dad's lover and then with his own reactions and feelings to a boy he meets at the ski resort.

Robbie Keeps the Key is also published by AuthorHouse.

Printed in the United States
By Bookmasters